Summer People

Summer People

L.H. FINIGAN

COBALT HOUSE

Cover painting: "Stonington, ME" by Rey Milici, Courtesy R. Michelson Galleries

"Everything That Was Broken" by Mary Oliver
Reprinted by the permission of The Charlotte Sheedy Literary Agency as agent for the author.
Copyright © 2015 by Mary Oliver with permission of Bill Reichblum

Book Design: Janis Owens
Editor: Elizabeth Foz

ISBN: 978-0-9829043-0-5

Library of Congress Control Number: 2025911584

Published by Cobalt House · PO Box 766 · Rockport, MA 01966

Printed in the United States of America

SummerPeopleNovel@gmail.com

Everything that was broken has forgotten its brokenness. I live now in a sky-house, through every window the sun

MARY OLIVER

Summer People

CHAPTER 1

Brilliant Boy

CATHARINE CONOR WAS EATING lunch in front of Widener Library when Tom Osborne bounded up the steps to join her. She was reading a book of poetry and had just taken a bite of her peanut butter sandwich when she looked up to see a tall man striding toward her, gesturing as though he already knew her. He wore a black sport coat and long white shirt, wire-rim glasses.

"Sorry," he called from a few steps away. "I just had to tell you—I love your skirt!"

Catharine was wearing a flowing orange pattern she'd fashioned from an Indian bedspread the night before. "Thanks. I made it."

"You make your own clothes?" The tone of his voice conveyed that she'd done something extraordinary.

"Sometimes."

"I didn't know people still did that!"

"Sure they do." Catharine had always enjoyed the accomplishment in creating something practical.

"You're reading Archie Dent," the man said, pointing to her book. "Don't you feel he's overrated? The whole male canon. The awards he's won. I don't think he's that great, do you? Standards don't exist anymore, no one cares, have you noticed? Or maybe you like his work? I don't mean to denigrate an idol."

Catharine laughed at this barrage of unsolicited opinion. The sun was in her eyes, blinding. Haloed by the light, he resembled a character in a movie she'd just seen. Sam Shepard, *Days of Heaven*. "He's asking the right questions, though," she said. "Don't you think?"

"Ah." Tom sat down beside her. "But does he have the answers?"

Catharine shifted her stack of books to give him room. She tucked her flowery skirt behind her knees. They talked on the library steps for the rest of her lunch hour until she told him she needed to return to her job at the Fogg. Tom said he'd been on his way to work, shelving books at Widener, but when he saw her from a distance, he knew they were meant to meet. Before they parted, he asked her to dinner that night at a nearby Indian restaurant. Over food that was too spicy to eat, they first discovered each other, the synchronicity of them, Catharine and Tom.

Tomcat he later christened them. After the first week, they were seldom apart. It was the summer of 1981, Prince Charles and Lady Di about to embark on their fairy tale, Catharine turning twenty. Everything seemed fated. She had sublet an apartment in Cambridge that summer. An art major at Simmons, she felt lucky to find a museum internship writing catalogues at the Fogg.

Tom was a poet, an editor of the graduate review. He was studying for his PhD at the same Harvard department where his father, a renowned Dante scholar, taught. Noah Osborne, or *Oddly Born*, as Tom dubbed him, also "Dr. NO," after his initials. His mother Polly he called "PO," signifying poor excuse for a mother. Catharine used to think everything Tom said about his parents must be comic exaggeration, until she met them and realized it wasn't.

For the rest of the summer, they spent every day together. Picnics on the Charles, lingering over the foreign papers at Out of Town News, inventing places they'd travel one day, pretending to speak Russian.

Tom likened Harvard Square's Garage shopping arcade to New York's Guggenheim, Catharine his audience of one, listening to his commentary as they ascended and descended the building's winding ramp. Tom invented stories about everyone they encountered—orange-haired skateboarders, street kids solemnly poking through bins of LPs in the record store, saffron-robed Hare Krishnas wafting incense, dancing up and down the spiral ramp, tambourines and song reverberating off the brick walls.

Catharine loved Tom from the start, his buoyant energy, his intellect. His recall of texts he'd read months or years before, the passion he brought to reciting passages from memory in those first dreamlike weeks of lying in bed for entire days, making love, drinking coffee or cheap jug wine. Thrilled by the intimacy of sharing secrets from their past, they spent days and nights talking. Whenever they parted, she couldn't wait for them to be together again.

Weekend nights when his parents were at their cottage on the Cape, they made love throughout the Osbornes' cavernous Brattle Street house—on the single bed in Tom's boyhood room, propped against the kitchen table, on the couch near the fireplace. One night, while searching for a bathroom down the hall, Catharine stood transfixed on the threshold of Dr. Osborne's study with its wood-paneled library and wall-to-wall shelves. To have a book-filled room like that to work in seemed beyond imagining, but then she felt Tom seeping out of her, and dashed the rest of the way down the hall.

Tom was sitting behind his father's desk when she passed the study door on her return.

"Come here," he said, beckoning.

Catharine shook her head. "Tom. We shouldn't."

"Yes, we should."

When Catharine went to sit on his lap, he wrapped his arms around her and spun them in circles in his father's leather chair before he came inside her. When they were still, Catharine held his face in her hands. She asked the question that only then occurred to her. "Why do you hate your father so much?"

Tom looked surprised. "Why would you say that?"

"The things you say—the joke you make about his initials—the way you argue."

"I don't hate him." Tom smiled, whirling them for another spin in Noah Osborne's swivel chair. "He hates me."

That week, she'd witnessed one of their father–son verbal duels for the first time, at dinner with Noah and Polly. Tom picked the place, Pentimento, a new favorite after a five-star review in the independent paper. Tom's choice of restaurant was the first thing he and his father argued about, followed by the aggravation of parking, the presumptuous attitude Tom felt in the way his father snapped his fingers, signaling the waitress. They debated an essay the elder Osborne had shown his son for editing, followed by Ronald Reagan and the war in El Salvador, various professors his father admired whom Tom despised, the weather. Catharine and Tom's mother averted their gaze to nearby diners. On the walk home, Tom said he wasn't upset. He didn't want to talk about it.

Catharine came to dread the weekly dinner with Tom's parents, the house that smelled vaguely of mothballs, Dr. Osborne waxing on about his research, his knowledge. Salvation and redemption in the world of Dante. Tom or his father invariably ended the evening enraged.

"That's ironic, isn't it?" Tom asked her after one interminable meal.

"What is?"

"His big theme. Do you think the old blowhard ever saved anybody? Do you think he gives a shit about anyone but himself?"

Summer turned hot. Neither of them had air conditioning. The day of the royal wedding, Tom and Catharine found a table at the Pamplona, a little basement space they loved, hoping for relief from the heat. They drank iced coffees, shared a cookie. Tom was sketching his vision for a communal arts center, an inspiration that had come to him fully formed the night before. Catharine felt carried away by his exuberance, his intellect, his plans for the future.

In the café, someone was listening to a replay of the day's events in London on a battery radio. The shop's faded sepia mural evoked Spain of another era; the tiled black-and-white floor seemed out of the thirties. On the street above, the Mass. Ave. bus thundered past on its way to Boston, the bell on the Catholic church across the street chimed each passing hour as Tom mapped out ideas with strokes of red felt pen on a napkin. He reached into an inside pocket for a second color to complete his design for a central meeting area, a dining room, salons for conversations; a lecture hall and performing arts center, the whole complex surrounded by concentric circles of cottages where all would live. Radical harmony. He outlined a nearby building for childcare, a community store, gallery space. Farming! They could support themselves by farming.

"We might have to move to a milder climate," Catharine ventured. "For farming."

"No, no. It can happen here. It already happened. Bronson Alcott, Emerson, the Transcendentalists!"

"I don't know that they succeeded at it, though, do you? Bronson Alcott—"

"A failed visionary," Tom agreed. "Yes. But none of them are forgotten. Is that failure?"

Catharine said of course it wasn't. You couldn't help but agree with Tom's enthusiasm when his words were fired by his zeal. She felt it, too, the possibilities he'd sketched out. She wanted that future. Later, they lay side by side on the grass along the Charles watching clouds chase across the sky, ascribing meaning to their shapes.

Schools of fish, a dinosaur, a fallen angel. A line came to Catharine, and she spoke it out loud. "The rage of being banished from heaven."

"What?" Tom said.

"That cloud up there with a shield and a spear. Wings. It looks like a fallen angel. The words just came to me, I don't know what they mean: *The rage of being banished from heaven*."

"And then? What's the next line?"

She thought for a moment. "I tremble for the earth."

"That could be a poem," Tom said. "That's the fragment of a poem. You should work on it."

"I'm not a poet," Catharine said.

"Yes, you are."

"You're the poet."

"I was."

His well-received chapbook when he was still an undergraduate. The editorship of the review, Tom at his desk bent over a notebook. The essence of who he was. She rolled on her side to throw an arm across his chest. "Yes you are. You'll always be. Our arts center poet-in-residence."

His expression darkened and she realized how mocking her voice sounded.

Catharine hugged him tighter. "You know I believe in you, right?"

"Why?" Tom said.

A week later, Catharine had just returned from a family wedding. Buddy, the cousin she'd had a crush on as a girl, had joined the Navy and married his high school sweetheart. When he was seventeen working behind the counter of her parents' deli in Queens, she used to fantasize they'd wind up together one day. She'd loved watching him, tall and slim in his white apron and T-shirt as her mother made potato salad behind the counter, her father sliced the meat. After school, Buddy used to make her egg cream sodas while she'd twirl on one of the counter stools, the bell jingling on the swinging door when customers came in. Sometimes, they were her elementary school classmates and then her father would allow her to give away a piece of candy as though she were bestowing gifts of the realm, a paper-wrapped brick of Mary Jane candy that would melt on your tongue, an Atomic Fireball. She'd sit on a stool, doing her homework watching Buddy make sandwiches, thinking she was in love.

Funny to think that once her girlhood crush on her cousin was what she'd dreamed of as love. She'd never really known what love was. Now she did. Every day she'd been away, Catharine missed Tom, wondering what he was doing that exact minute. She'd phoned his apartment twice, but he didn't answer. Now she looped an arm through his as they walked beside the river. "Have you done anything more towards the arts center?"

Tom looked momentarily bewildered. "What?" It took him a beat to realize what she was talking about. He laughed. "The arts center. Like that's ever going to happen."

Catharine stopped but he kept walking. "Why isn't it going to happen?" she called after him.

"For one thing, it's way too complicated. I mean—really? I'm going to build an arts center?" He slowed when she caught up with him. "I get carried away sometimes."

"But Tom, it was a great idea," she went on. "It was the perfect place. I would have lived there."

"You'd have been miserable."

Catharine stood still. "Tell me what happened, what changed."

"It wouldn't work. It was never going to work. It only seemed like it might because you were listening."

Catharine wouldn't let it go. "The way you brought those plans to life, I could see it. It was a beautiful idea, Tom. It still is."

He smiled and kissed her hand. "So are they all, beautiful ideas."

"I could help you."

He raised a hand to her cheek and pulled her close, but this time he didn't move to kiss her. "Catharine." He stared into her eyes. "Stop."

Sun glistened on the river; a bullhorn sounded from one of the rowing skiffs shooting past. Skaters and cyclists wove around them. They stood holding each other for what seemed a long time. She felt his body shudder. He drew back, his hands resting on her shoulders. "Anyway, you were right," he said. "I'd make a terrible farmer."

Summer was ending, the new semester about to begin.

Tom always wrote his poems by hand in notebooks purchased from Bob Slate's, a little stationery store near Mt. Auburn. The notebooks, he'd told her, had to be the same thickness, dimension, and color. She'd seen them lined up on the bookshelf in his bedroom. Sometimes he'd take a volume down and read her something he'd written. The week before classes started, Catharine went with him to buy another. She was happy to think he was working on something new.

A middle-aged man in shirtsleeves delivered the news. "They've stopped making those, sir."

"They've stopped making them?" Tom sounded offended. "A special order then?"

"I'm sorry. There's no way to order more."

"There has to be a way."

"We've checked with the manufacturer. I'm afraid there isn't."

"That can't be. You don't understand," Tom insisted. "I need to have that notebook. I can't work without it."

"It's a notebook!" Catharine said. "It's not magic, Tom. Your powers won't vanish without the right notebook."

He turned to her. "It's more than the notebook, Cat. It's the ritual. My ritual. I can't explain."

"I think it's silly."

"You can't say that to an artist."

Catharine laughed. "Please."

Later, he sat with his head in his hands on a bench in the park. "You don't understand how terrible this is. You don't understand."

"I guess I don't."

Tom remained with shoulders hunched. He didn't look up. Finally she understood. "Tom, are you crying? Tell me what's wrong. Is it because of the notebook?"

"It's not the notebook." He looked up at her with anguish. "I'm under an incredible amount of pressure, Cat."

"Why? It's still summer. Classes haven't started."

"Not school. I'm not talking about school."

"Then what?"

"Something happened," he said.

"What?"

He looked down at the grass. "They asked me to step down."

"Who?"

Tom shook his head.

Catharine still didn't know what he was talking about. "Who did?"

"The editorial board asked me to resign," he said. "They made me step down."

"Why?"

"Don't you know?" Tom's eyes searched hers. Calmly he said, "Because I'm crazy."

She thought he was joking.

"Tom, you're scaring me a little."

He held his face in his hands and was silent for a long while. Finally he sat up straight and turned to face her. "Don't be scared." The fear in his eyes was gone. She watched him pull himself together, the agitation dissipating, like an actor transitioning before her eyes. "I get this way sometimes," he said. "And then I'm fine. Really. You don't need to be afraid."

"Okay," Catharine said tentatively. She rested her hand on his.

When she thought the episode had passed, he leaned against her shoulder and whispered, "You know you deserve someone else."

They saw each other less often once September arrived, classes underway. Catharine's dorm at Simmons in the Fenway was a long subway and bus ride from Tom's place in Harvard Square. Often when she called his apartment, the phone rang unanswered even when she knew he must be there.

One night in early November, Catharine met a friend in Harvard Square. After a movie at the Brattle, she decided on a whim to surprise Tom at work, the way he would sometimes show up unannounced that summer at the museum.

She knew something was wrong as soon as she came through the Mass. Ave. gate. Police and fire engines surrounded Widener Library, their flashing blue and red lights blinding in the dark. The building was being evacuated, students and professors pouring down the front steps where, months earlier, she and Tom had met. She didn't see flames or smell smoke. She thought it must be a bomb threat, a false alarm.

In the distance, she spotted Tom in the crowd, wild-eyed, frantic. When she ran up to tap his shoulder, he whirled around with an expression of panic. "Oh my God. Cat. What are you doing here?"

"I just—thought I'd surprise you." Catharine wished now she hadn't. She could be on the subway home, not a witness to whatever had happened here, Tom disintegrating before her.

"You have to leave," he ordered. He ran a hand through his hair, standing it on end, as though a current had passed through him. "Do you understand? You can't be here now."

"Tom, what happened? What's wrong?"

"There's been a fire. *I set a fire*," is what she thought he said, but how could that be true.

"What did you do?"

"I don't know," he cried. "You have to go."

"Tom—"

He held her by the shoulders; his gaze drilled through her. "Go," he said. "Go home. I'll call you."

Catharine backed away. Beneath the brick archway to Mass. Ave. she looked over her shoulder in hopes of finding him again, but Tom had been swallowed by the crowd.

He was arrested the next morning, caught on a security camera as he set a small blaze in the stacks that housed his father's books. Catharine was seized by an irrational fear that she'd never see him again. What would happen if his father wouldn't post bail? But he did. Noah Osborne got his son released. Catharine wondered if he ever knew that the books Tom had burned were ones he'd written.

She was waiting on the porch of Tom's apartment when he emerged from a cab early the next morning. Unshaven, his wrinkled shirt untucked, his hair needing combing. "Catharine!" He bounded up the stairs to fold her in his arms.

"I thought maybe I'd never see you again."

"Of course you'd see me again."

"But if I didn't?"

"I'll never let that happen," he said. "I love you, Cat."

It was the first time he'd said those words. She echoed them in return. As damaged as Tom was, maybe would always be, she loved him. She didn't want to lose him. She needed Tom in her life. They needed each other.

They stumbled up the stairs like drunks, shedding their clothes as soon as Tom shut the door. He leaned against her, the weight of his body pressing them to the door. The love they made that early morning was otherworldly, transformational, the sky ablaze with a wintry sunrise beyond the curtains of his third-floor room. Despite her doubts, what could that mean but a resounding yes from the universe. Yes!

"I'm so sorry," he kept repeating. "I'm so sorry, Cat. I'll do better. I will."

"I know you will," Catharine said quietly. "I know."

She didn't have her diaphragm that morning. What were the chances? It didn't matter.

When she learned she was pregnant, the first thought was not to believe it. How could it be true. She'd dropped the still-warm jar of urine at the clinic that morning. The detached voice on the phone that afternoon announced, "Your test was positive," as though this was a fact without consequence. Catharine sat down. No, that couldn't be. It was unreal, too fast, something you should be able to undo, rewind, a dream that would vanish once you woke. A baby? Such a monumental consequence to the act of making love. Maybe it wasn't love at all they'd been making, but responsibility, commitment, a thousand things neither she nor Tom were ready for, but now she was pregnant.

When she dreamt of the baby a few nights later, it was as though her body had already made its choice. In the dream, she'd finally given in to the voices telling her she was too young to have a baby. "There's another option, you know," friends advised. She dreamt she was an old woman, her hair white. She wore a colorful satiny robe like the Beatles in Sgt. Pepper, her ancient self lying on a bed with her hair spread around her, and in the dream, she wanted her daughter to be with her. In the dream, she knew she'd made the wrong decision.

When she told Tom later that week over coffee at their café, he said, "It's not like you can actually have a baby, can you?" His tone supplied its own answer.

"Why can't I?"

"How?" he countered.

"It's not impossible, Tom."

"It seems impossible," he said. "Look at me, Cat. Sometimes I'm a wreck. Sometimes I'm okay. I'm not a father. You know that."

"I don't."

"I won't let you throw your life away."

What if I already have? crossed her mind, but she didn't say it. "It's not up to you," she said.

"I don't have a say?"

"I'll do it on my own. You can't order me what to do."

Catharine stared at him coldly. Her decision solidified in that moment. Maybe she would ruin her life, but she would have the baby. She couldn't explain why it seemed beyond argument, as though she had no choice. For the first time in her life, she felt herself in the power of something beyond herself.

Tom leaned forward across the table. He took her by the shoulders. "A baby? Are you crazy?"

"You should leave."

"Catharine—"

"I mean it. We can't talk about this now. You should go."

Tom grabbed his keys and loudly pushed back his chair. "I can't believe you'd do this."

He showed up that night outside her dorm window, rapping on the glass with an open bottle. He must have climbed the fire escape. He was kneeling on the steel balcony. Catharine thought of Romeo and Juliet. She opened the window and crawled outside beside him. "Are you drunk?"

"Harvard threw me out," he said.

A single star shone overhead. To the east, a plane descended into Logan; the traffic light at the corner blinked from yellow to red.

"For good?"

"I think so." Tom offered her the bottle and she shook her head. "They're not pressing charges, but in return ..." His voice drifted away. He took a long swig and wiped his mouth with his sleeve. "Dr. NO worked his voodoo. I can finish my degree at King's College. I don't know how he set that up. What do you think? Do you want to go to London? Want to share my bright future as an arsonist?"

"That's not funny."

"Of course it's not."

It seemed another lifetime that they'd sat in the basement of the Café Pamplona, listening to snippets of the royal wedding, Tom sketching his manic arts center idea on a napkin. London had seemed magical then.

"When will you go?"

"Soon."

"And us?"

"Come with me," Tom begged. "That's what I came to say. I can change, Cat. I'll change. Just be with me. I need you in my life."

"And the baby?"

"I'm sorry about what I said before. Whatever you want. We'll make it work."

She wanted to believe they had a future, that Tom would be okay.

They arranged a small wedding. Tom's mother insisted they have a lavish engagement party. "*Before you show.*" Polly Osborne patted Catharine's stomach as though having a child were something they'd planned, a reason to celebrate.

Late in the evening, Tom's father tapped his flute until the room fell silent and then he began reciting a long passage on the sorrows of love from Dante. No dedication or congratulations to the engaged couple. Catharine watched the faces of their friends register first polite interest, then bemusement, finally derision. The monologue dragged on. When Catharine caught Polly's eye, her future mother-in-law dropped her gaze to the floor. Catharine wondered how many nights Tom's mother must have witnessed this performance, faculty dinners, family holidays, other people's weddings. She imagined that even when he was young, the dazzling Dr. Osborne must have regaled whatever crowd he found himself in with favorite passages from Dante. Catharine assumed he must be drunk, but Tom told her later that he wasn't. He'd seen it before.

At the little wedding a week later, Polly took Catharine aside. She clasped her new daughter-in-law's hands in her own ringed ones.

"It's up to you now." Polly Osborne spoke in a tone that was not a request. "We're all counting on you, Catharine. Keep our brilliant boy safe."

"I'll try," Catharine offered, too startled to say anything else. "I'll do my best."

But what about me? Even then, on the first night of her marriage, before she grasped all that would be asked of her, Catharine knew that was the question. Who takes care of me?

In their little London flat above a lunch shop near campus, she thought of Sylvia Plath. The cold of winter, the warmth of the gas oven in the little kitchen. Alone at the dining table, typing up Tom's thesis, she waited for him to return from his day of classes, his evening job shelving books at the library where no one had bothered to check his record in the States. Tom was proud of his service, his atonement for the fire at Widener. He worked at the library!

When her new husband returned in the evening, he was often moody, withdrawn, annoyed. Not the company she'd waited for. He was annoyed with his day, Catharine told herself, not at her. She was careful not to upset him, always trying to make things right for Tom, to keep things light so that their baby would arrive in peace and her husband would not pitch sideways off the cliff of his life a second time.

In February, she had a miscarriage.

When Tom arrived at the emergency department where she'd taken herself by bus, the first words he blurted out were, "Oh, thank God."

She hoped that meant he was grateful she was okay, but he went on. "It's for the best, isn't it? What kind of parents would we be? How could we have a baby?"

Catharine rolled away from his touch, the tears she'd swallowed flowing finally. "How can you say that to me?"

"Cat—"

"Please go."

"Catharine."

"I can't talk about it now." She pushed him away. "I need you to go." She turned her face to the wall, crying because it was a relief for her, too. She didn't want to admit that, because she'd wanted the baby, she really did. But Tom was right. Neither of them were ready. They needed to finish school. They needed so many things.

At home, in their depressing flat above the shop, Catharine began writing. At first, it was raw emotion, what she might have poured out to Tom if she hadn't been so angry, or a friend, if she'd had any in this cold, wet foreign country. Soon, her words became something else. Paragraphs distilled to a phrase, an image, a sentence.

A lifeline.

CHAPTER 2

The House on Fairview Road

THE FIRST DAY SHE SAW IT, Catharine fell in love with the house. Its big bay window and painted shutters, the red maple out front, the towering willow next door, a glimpse of sea visible through trees. She would always love it, an attachment outweighing its state of repair. A love of the house and its surroundings that helped, in years to come, to make up for no longer loving Tom the way she hoped she would, the way she'd imagined married love would be when she was doodling wedding dresses in three-ring notebooks when she should have been learning algebra.

Catharine pictured everything the house could become the first time she saw it, though it never quite became all she'd envisioned. They never had the money. Tom didn't really love the house, but he loved the town, Belle Harbor, its remoteness on a tip of land north of Boston where no one would ever drop by unexpected. Especially his parents.

Catharine had visited the place once before when she was ten. The drive up from Queens had seemed endless—first through parkways and over bridges, then upstate and along a twisting path through Connecticut into Massachusetts—her father behind the wheel of his Impala. From the balcony of their beach motel, they watched the moon rise over the Atlantic. Her frugal mother allowed them to splurge on ice cream and salt water taffy. When they went out to eat, it wasn't for pizza. Catharine discovered the summer meal she loved most, tartar sauce on sizzling clams fresh from the fryer.

Rachel and Jimmy Conor rarely took vacations since that meant closing the deli or hiring someone to run it in their absence. In her father's opinion, a few days off was never worth the complaints. Customers told Rachel that without her, the potato salad had too much mayo, the ham was sliced too thin. Maybe Belle Harbor seemed magical to Catharine—or Kitty as she was called then—because for once her parents weren't tethered to the store.

Seeing it again as an adult, she had no idea why she'd never taken the train up from Boston in all the time she'd lived in the city as a student. One hot August afternoon, a few years after London, she persuaded Tom to leave their cramped third-floor walk-up and go with her.

A picturesque stroll brought them from the train station into town. Passing a realtor's window, Catharine stopped to look at flyers. There it was. The house on Fairview Road. Four bedrooms including the one in the attic, two baths, seasonal ocean views, the cheapest listing in the window.

"That's because there's something wrong with it," Tom pointed out when she expressed surprise at the price. "There has to be."

"Can't we at least walk by?"

They hadn't been looking for a house; they'd been looking for real jobs. Everyone told them they were wasting their dwindling savings on a tiny Comm. Ave. apartment that was more than they could afford. They had yet to find permanent work. Catharine was a part-time secretary; Tom did copy editing.

A short walk up the coast, they came to the street, Fairview Road. Catharine laughed. "Even the name, Tom!"

"Better than Crummy Vista," he allowed.

Seen from the curb, it was clear the place needed work. The garden was overgrown. A few shingles were missing. "Let's go back and tell the realtor we want to see it," Catharine said.

"You can't be serious."

"At least take a look? We're here for the day. We haven't found anything in Boston. What if we found work here instead? I could be a waitress up here as easily as the city, a temp secretary until we found something. You could be a substitute teacher."

"Catharine, I have a PhD."

"I know that."

In the end, she persuaded him they could at least have a look.

"You're going to love this place," the realtor raved as she unlocked the door. Bottle blonde and cheerful, her name was Dee. "All it needs is a little elbow grease and imagination!"

Tom and Catharine hung back on the threshold. Her first impression was of echoing rooms and the musty smell of a shuttered house. The realtor's heels clattered through the halls.

A single feather blew across the living room in the breeze, Dee exclaiming, "Look at this open floor plan."

Out of earshot, Tom issued a verdict. "We can't afford it, Cat." He was firm. "The house is a wreck. Nobody's done upkeep for at least ten years."

On the second floor, Dee opened what looked like a hall closet but led to a narrow staircase. "And here's the bonus!" she gushed. "A finished attic bedroom!"

Catharine saw herself locked away up there, scribbling in one of the notebooks she'd purchased in a bookshop near the British Museum. She'd yet to write a word since the anguished outpouring of pages after the baby, but in her attic room she thought she could.

"I'll leave you two alone to confer." The realtor quietly retreated down the stairs.

Catharine made her decision in that moment. "We have to buy this house, Tom," she said.

Her husband sighed. "The plumbing's old. I bet the wiring is old. Look at the faucets."

"We can clean them."

"The guest room toilet seat's cracked."

"That's ten dollars. Twenty? Tom, look at this place. Come here."

Catharine grabbed him by one arm and pulled him to the east-facing window, raising her face to his. His expression betrayed a reluctant sense of duty: after everything he'd put her through, how could he disappoint her in this?

"That's a lighthouse through the branches." She pointed in the distance, a white tower blinking beside an old lightkeeper's house. A green light swung into view, then disappeared to return a few seconds later. "There's an actual sliver of ocean through the trees. In the winter, this will be beautiful."

"The house is a wreck," Tom said again.

"I'll make the down payment. The money from my aunt." Catharine had inherited a small sum the year before. She'd put it aside to use someday on her own. *Your Virginia Woolf account,* Tom teasingly named it. "Five thousand dollars," she reminded him, no longer a hint of question in her voice. "That's our down payment."

They'd seen the place in summer but it was winter by the time they moved in, the trees leafless, the garden gone. Catharine tried to remember what had been blooming so lushly in August when they first saw the house, but she couldn't. She was right about the view from their bedroom window, though. Every time she glimpsed it, the ocean beyond their window was a surprise.

Across the gravel driveway was their nearest neighbor, a little cottage closed for the season. Plywood shutters covered the windows facing the sea. A vacation house. She hoped for a quiet couple reading books, sipping wine on the deck.

Catharine claimed the little dormer in the attic as her work room. Tom said he'd be happy with the spare room on the second floor. Catharine felt as though they'd acquired a castle, to have gone from their confined few rooms to the luxury of space. Maybe here on Fairview Road Tom would finally get back to writing. Once or twice she'd seen him with a notebook, but she didn't want to ask if he was working again.

Catharine was carrying boxes up the attic stairs one day after they'd moved in when a carton slipped from her hands, scattering paper down the steps. As she knelt to retrieve folders, her eye fell on a strange seam beneath the bottom stair. A drawer.

She jiggled it open to find a stack of *Life* magazines from the sixties. She flipped through the familiar covers remembered from childhood. JFK's assassination, the moon landing, the Beatles.

Beneath the magazines were a stack of letters and a wallet. The wallet was empty save for an ancient foil-wrapped condom. Most of the letters were addressed to "Jim." Who was Jim? Was the wallet his? One envelope had a return address on Marlborough Street in Boston, not far from where she and Tom used to live. The envelopes bore no stamps. It appeared none had ever been sent.

The first was handwritten in graceful blue ink. It was dated the twenty-eighth of August, almost two decades before.

Dear Jim,

Of course you're not here tonight, the night our son died.

"Oh God," Catharine said out loud. She felt a chill sweep down the attic stairs as though she'd been caught spying. She quickly refolded the cream-colored paper and fitted it back into its envelope, then shuffled the letter deeper into the pile. She hesitated, but then opened another.

I don't know why I'm writing you these thoughts. If you were here tonight, I wouldn't speak them. Why write them in a letter I'll probably never send? I never do. Tonight you're in Chicago, concluding some deal as I sit here after the children are asleep, realizing that when you're away, as you often are, I no longer miss you. I prefer it. The silence is easier to bear when you're a thousand miles away.

Catharine slid the letter back into its envelope. She flipped through the rest on her lap. Two were addressed to Kyle, but she couldn't bring herself to open those. Without reading a word, she knew that Kyle would be their dead son. The wallet must be his.

For days, Catharine debated what to do. She could contact the real estate agent and tell her what she'd found beneath the stairs, but in the end, she wrote a letter addressed to *Belle Harbor Summer House* in care of the Marlborough Street address. When a reply arrived in the mail, Catharine recognized the handwriting from the letters beneath the stairs.

Her name was Emma Nolan.

Thank you so much for letting me know about the letters. Yes, I would love to have them back. Perhaps you and your husband would like to come for lunch in Boston one day? I would very much enjoy meeting the young couple who bought our house!

Tom had no interest in the woman who once lived in their house. Catharine took the train back to the city herself, the first time she'd taken the rail since the day they rode up to Belle Harbor the previous summer, the morning she first discovered Fairview Road.

Scenery flew by. Three-story houses huddled close to the tracks in the harbor town of New Vernon. Sprawling mansions followed down the coast before a string of commuter towns emptied into the industrial sprawl of Boston, a steel and glass skyline above colonial brick.

A garden with a wrought-iron fence surrounded Emma Nolan's brownstone on Marlborough Street, a tulip tree blooming outside a bay window, a planter of pussy willows and daffodils underneath. Catharine was buzzed in.

An ornate staircase led to the second floor. Catharine knocked. When the apartment door opened, the woman who stood there looked much as Catharine pictured her, silver hair in a bun, interested blue eyes. She was taller than Catharine imagined, wearing an apron. The apartment smelled of chocolate.

"Would you like a glass of wine?" the woman asked after she showed Catharine to a seat in the living room. A table at the window was set for lunch, two salads arranged on plates.

Catharine thought her face must have registered surprise.

"It's not too early, is it?" Emma asked.

Catharine laughed. "Not for me. Not at all."

"Let's be festive then."

Emma went into the kitchen and returned with two glasses of white. Catharine reached into her bag and withdrew the parcel she'd wrapped in brown paper. She hoped she'd be gone when Emma opened the letters. "These are for you."

"Gosh. So large," Emma said, before settling the package beside her on the couch.

"There were a few *Life* magazines, too."

Emma smiled. "My son's magazines. I'd forgotten."

Catharine didn't know how to respond. After a pause, Emma stood and announced, "Let's have lunch!" The casserole dish that emerged from the kitchen smelled like one that Catharine's mother might have cooked.

Over lunch, Emma asked what had brought a young couple to a place like Belle Harbor and Catharine explained how she'd visited long ago as a child and how they really hadn't been looking to buy a house, though they needed to move out of their stifling, ridiculously priced space, how she'd fallen in love with the house the moment she saw it.

That made Emma smile. "I'm so glad. I didn't want to give it up, but—" Her voice trailed off. "It was time."

"What you have here is quite beautiful," Catharine hurried to add. "Your apartment. Tom and I would have gladly stayed in Boston if we had this much space!"

"My husband was in banking. I can't remember how he heard when the building went on the market." Emma gazed out the window. "One of his good decisions." She laughed. "You can't imagine how little it cost us then. Back in the fifties. I'm embarrassed to think what we paid."

She got up to clear the plates. Catharine offered to help but Emma said she was fine. "Do you like chocolate?" she asked.

"I love chocolate. I was hoping that smell when you opened the door meant dessert."

Emma brought out a plate of brownies on a china plate.

"Oh," Catharine sighed when she'd sampled one, dense and dark. Delicious. "I've never tasted such a great brownie."

Emma beamed. "Special recipe. Do you have children? I'd love to give it to you."

Catharine wondered what her face conveyed then. To her embarrassment, she felt tears flood her eyes. "We don't have children." The hospital in London, Tom patting her feebly on the back, telling her it was for the best, wasn't it?

She could have left him then, but she didn't.

She knew Emma spotted her tears.

"Well." The older woman reached out to hold Catharine's hand. "In the end," she said, "sometimes they break your heart."

CHAPTER 3

Paradise

IT QUICKLY BECAME APPARENT that the house required far more work than they'd imagined. Walls and ceilings needed painting, floors had to be sanded, each room a revelation of something else that would soon demand costly repair. Still, Belle Harbor made up for it. Its coves and beaches, hidden paths; tidal pools and cliffs overlooking the sea, an even more magical place than Catharine had remembered as a child. Sitting on their deck at night, she and Tom watched the planes heading out over the Atlantic, made wishes on the stars blinking into view. She couldn't believe their good fortune. They'd found a home by the sea.

Jobs eventually followed, the future Catharine imagined standing before the realtor's window that first summer morning. She was hired as a maternity leave substitute for an art teacher a few towns away. Tom's father used his connections to get him a job teaching at a community college near Boston. The commute would be long, but Tom could read or grade papers on the train. Besides, it was all temporary. They'd get better jobs. What mattered was to have found their stake in paradise.

When the new mother Catharine subbed for decided not to return, the school district offered her a permanent job as middle school art teacher. Not how she'd imagined using her art history degree, but she was happy. Catharine grew to love the smells of the art room, glue and acrylics, oil and charcoal. The joy of the children.

Tom didn't love teaching, but he told her he was glad to make the sacrifice. He claimed it was worth it to see her happy, to share her childlike delight in discovering the house, the garden, the town. One night, he went so far as to say the house was worth everything they had, to see her emerge from the shadow of losing the baby. Here was their second chance. He vowed to do better.

And he did change. A familiar euphoria was rising in him. He told Catharine he could feel the same unstoppable energy that had fueled him before, those times in his life when he'd accomplished the most—the years he was the golden boy in high school, when he'd published his small chapbook as an undergraduate and earned his father's grudging praise, when he became editor of the graduate journal at Harvard, and when they first met, when he'd seen his best self reflected back in her love.

Catharine saw that whirlwind of hope and possibility take hold of him again their first year in Belle Harbor. He sanded cabinet doors in the basement at 5 a.m. when he couldn't sleep, ripped up carpeting at midnight. Later, she thought if she'd been paying closer attention, she would have seen Tom's frenzy of home repair for what it was, the foreshadowing of another descent into the dark.

They'd bought a four-bedroom house, large enough for a family. No children arrived. Still, Catharine was content with her summers free from teaching, time that would allow her to write, the beauty of Belle Harbor, the equilibrium she and Tom had somehow managed to carve after their early years.

On a June day in their second year in the house Catharine came across a familiar name in the village paper. Emma Nolan had died. The obituary listed an upcoming memorial on Boylston Street in Boston. Catharine knew she had to go.

Tom didn't want to go to a funeral, though it was a day he'd already be in town teaching. Catharine realized she was grateful to go alone to the courtyard of the Boston Public Library, a space she'd always loved. She used to sit in that courtyard listening to the fountain, surrounded by arched columns and flower beds, scribbling in her journal. The courtyard had been her outdoor retreat from the apartment on Comm. Ave.

Photos of Emma Nolan and her family lined the walkways. Pots of flowers looked like they'd been brought from people's gardens, baskets of rhododendron and roses. Catharine lingered at the photos of the house when it was newly built, the trees and shrubs barely grown. Emma as a young woman with long blonde hair, Emma and Jim, Emma and her children when they were babies; Emma in all the stages of her life. Clad in an apron in the kitchen of Fairview Road, smiling as she turned from the oven with a tray of cookies; Emma and her young son seated by a lake. Catharine thought of the letters hidden beneath the stairs. *Sometimes they break your heart.*

Servers in black vests circulated trays of hors d'oeuvres and champagne. A cellist played music in an alcove with lovely acoustics. Catharine knew without asking that all this would have been Emma's instructions. At the end of the afternoon a young woman, whose hair was as blonde as Emma's had been, greeted people as they drifted away. She was Emma's daughter.

"I don't think we've met."

"Catharine Osborne. My husband and I bought your mother's house in Belle Harbor."

"Oh, the delightful young couple!" Diana laughed but there was a strange edge in her tone. From the obituary, Catharine knew she lived in India. Was she not close with her mother? "She talked about you."

"She did?"

"On the phone. She loved meeting you, that time you came for lunch in Boston. She was so thrilled that a young couple starting out would settle on Fairview Road. I never understood what she loved about that house."

"I love it, too."

"That would have made her happy," Diana said.

After she left, Catharine carried the warm glow of Emma Nolan's life with her through the city, heading for the train where Tom was saving a seat for her on the five o'clock. The night was mild. She decided to walk to North Station.

Whatever her tragedies, Emma's life seemed one well lived. Catharine would be grateful to have the same someday. How glad she was to have discovered that hidden drawer in the attic stairs which led to her meeting the woman, if only once.

Tom lifted his eyes from his book when she took the seat beside him on the train. "So did the old gal leave you anything in her will?" he asked.

Catharine stared back in disbelief, her mood shattered, Tom's careless cold humor puncturing the lovely thoughts she'd woven from the afternoon. She turned toward the window.

"What?" he asked.

Catharine refused to answer. They rode the rest of the way in silence.

At home in the kitchen, she made herself a peanut butter sandwich and carried it upstairs to the attic.

"So that's it?" Tom called after her up the stairs.

In her attic room, Catharine shut the door and did something she hadn't managed in years. She emptied herself into a poem.

In time, when people asked, she'd tell them that the words that brought them comfort, the poem they read at their mothers' memorials, "Emma's Kitchen," wrote itself.

CHAPTER 4

Summer People

SOMETIMES SHE FORGETS what awaits upon her annual return to the house on Fairview Road, the weekend place she and Jim bought when the children were small, memories springing like surprise guests the moment she opens the door.

Emma Nolan steps inside her son's old bedroom and hesitates. Something still smells of him here. His aftershave, the cologne he wore in high school? After a moment's pause, she strides through the room, throwing open windows. Kyle, her youngest, the cleverest of the two, the one closest to her heart, the surprise when she was already forty-four.

Kyle slept beneath the window in the back bedroom. Diana, four years older, occupied the canopy bed against the wall those summers they shared the same room. At night when she read to them, Diana was the listener. Kyle occupied himself with Legos or Matchbox cars, but Emma knew he was secretly paying attention. The questions he asked, always the most analytical. Jim's sharp intelligence in the body of a five-year-old.

In the corner of the kitchen, a huge rattan chair remains where her son had placed it, imposing as a throne. He'd been so thrilled to scavenge it somewhere, carting it home on his back, a half mile from town. He must have been ten, always tall for his age. Kyle liked to read curled up in that chair while she baked, his long legs folded beneath him.

Long before Jim started doing well at the bank, Emma had a little baked goods business, Sweet Endings, catering to the inns and a few shops in town, what people now called *gourmet*. Her recipe for triple chocolate brownies was a legend in Belle Harbor. She used to wear a purple apron, Diana balanced on a stool, asking to lick the beaters. In the window, Emma catches her true reflection, a woman of seventy-nine, her hair once faithfully dyed blonde now silvery white at last, a handsome woman, as she has always been.

A flat of petunias are waiting on her porch, ready to be planted. She'd stopped at the nursery on her way into town, her yearly arrival tradition. Kneeling by the mailbox garden, Emma carefully unwraps root balls, loosening compacted ones, whispering encouragement as she settles petunias into the earth. She doesn't imagine flowers understand; still she thinks it's the secret of what has made her garden beautiful all these years. Living things need to know you appreciate their presence. She pats the last blossom into the ground, telling it to thrive, just as a young jogger emerges from behind the hedge. He must have heard. She'd become a batty old lady talking to her plants. That was fine. Emma gathers her gardening bucket. Steadying herself against the post, she gets to her feet, slower than she was last year, the toll of another winter.

When she was in grade school, Emma and a friend used to giggle in derision at an old woman they often passed when they got off the bus. All these years later, she feels guilty about that, even if it was Emma's friend, Jo, who was the instigator. Emma always laughed, too. An old woman walking her Pomeranian every day, lipstick applied as an estimate of where lips might be, pats of rouge like round tomatoes on each cheek, arched black eyebrows penciled on, her white hair askew beneath a purple beret. It was the gash of lipstick that set Jo and Emma off, elbowing each other and snickering as their neighbor passed, not always out of earshot. That woman seemed so old to them then. Emma is practically her age.

Now Emma's daughter lives on the other side of the planet. India, where the husband Emma never liked scouts international businesses for an investment firm, a promotion two years ago which everyone but Emma seemed to agree couldn't possibly be turned down. Her daughter saw a move across the globe as a great adventure, as Emma probably would have, too, when she was thirty-seven.

At Diana's age, she and Jim were childless, her daughter born when she was forty. The doctors discouraged another, but Emma didn't listen. Whenever she encounters a woman her age now, a pack of grandchildren in tow, Emma wonders if there was anything she could have done differently for Diana to turn out less dependent on someone else's choices, ready to be pulled this way or that, all the way to India in the end, following her husband's ambition. She and her daughter spoke once a week by phone; they wrote letters that took weeks to arrive. Was her daughter happy? Emma had no idea.

That night, Emma watches for a light at Maureen O'Malley's, wondering if her friend is back yet from winter in Manhattan. Every year when she returns to Belle Harbor, Emma looks forward to picking up where they left off the previous fall. Since they both lost their husbands years ago, she and Maureen have steadily extended their summer stays well past September. A little cottage lies in between their adjacent houses, occupied now on occasional summer weekends by far-flung children and grandchildren. Maureen's late husband built it twenty years before.

Later than usual, a light finally comes on inside the house beyond the cottage, though not in Maureen's bedroom. Emma will visit in the morning.

When she knocks on the door, a loaf of fresh-baked zucchini bread still warm in her hands, Maureen's son Paul is the one to greet her. His face freezes when he sees Emma. "Oh my God, I'm so sorry."

"What?" Emma leans against the screen door.

"I didn't know how to reach her summer friends up here. I'm sorry. I should have let you know but—My mother died of a stroke this winter."

"Oh." Emma feels the wind knocked from her lungs. All these months, laughing Maureen O'Malley was not in her New York apartment mixing martinis as Emma liked to picture her. She was dead and Emma didn't know.

"I'm sorry," her son says again.

"No, it's—" Emma struggles for words. "It's not your fault. You had a lot to think about. It's hard to lose someone. You lost your mother."

Paul's expression hasn't changed. He stares at his feet. "Nothing compared to the loss you've been through."

Emma shakes her head. "Even if you wrote me up here—they hold my mail. It's never anything besides catalogues. I'm just—" She feels herself about to cry. "Thank you for letting me know. I'm so sorry. Here." She thrusts the loaf into his hands. "Zucchini bread."

Maureen's son startles back to life. "There was a memorial service in February," he says. "Let me get you a program. I brought some in case I ran into anyone she knew."

Emma waits at the door while he retrieves it from deep inside the house. On the cover, there's a smiling color photo of her friend, a picture Emma took the previous summer, the late evening sun in Maureen O'Malley's face beneath her yellow sun hat, martini glass lifted in a toast. No plastic cup of wine for Maureen O'Malley. She always brought her own martini shaker and glass to summer parties.

Leaving the house, Emma turns left instead of right toward home. She wanders dazed to the end of the street, the outcropping of rocks that overlook the ocean. Sometimes she and Maureen came here to watch the sky change colors at sunset. Now Emma sits alone, staring out across a flat sea, a leaden sky. She toasts the horizon. "Cheers, old friend."

She tries not to blame Maureen's family when she learns they've decided to rent the little cottage next door by the week that summer. Now that the matriarch is gone, the family won't be coming up for summers anymore. Eventually they'd probably sell it but for now why not a summer rental. Sitting on her front porch looking at the stars one Friday evening, Emma sees a car slowly cruise down Fairview Road to pull into the drive next door.

They've arrived, the first new tenants of the season. The summer people. Of course, she's a summer person too, as she's always been, though she never thinks of herself that way. She's been spending practically half the year in Belle Harbor for so long, Emma thinks of herself as a townie. She hears the laughter of a child. They have children.

When Diana and her husband moved to India, taking Emma's two little granddaughters with them, she thought nothing would ever fill the hole they left behind. To lose her friend this year as well—Emma doesn't know what she'll do all summer.

Much to her surprise, the rented cottage turns out to provide a steady turnover of weekly drama. It's almost like going to the movies. On holiday from their real lives, Emma imagines they're different people from who they are at home, inhibitions loosened, constraints removed, an endless parade of human fascination.

It becomes a Friday ritual. Car doors thrown open, luggage carried in. If it's daylight, the fathers investigate the grill first, stopping to examine it critically, lifting the black hood to peer inside, trying controls. Snippets of conversations rise from the back deck. Some tenants keep the bathroom light on all night; others, the one on the porch, which shines in Emma's bedroom window. She wonders what kind of places they've come from. Have they spent their whole lives afraid of the dark?

This Saturday morning, there's a new family eating breakfast on the deck, two blonde little girls and an older boy. The girls wear pink pajamas, short hair rustling in the wind. They clamber onto their father's lap. Emma remembers how Diana used to fall asleep intently sucking her thumb. She always did this with concentrated purpose, stroking her nose for added comfort. When Emma glances out the kitchen window, both girls are descending the deck stairs, singing to themselves.

Captivated, Emma awakes the next morning with a plan. What if she baked something again to deliver to the family next door? Maybe she could do so all summer, a way to stay busy. Meet new people. She thinks of the visit from the Welcome Wagon when she was a child after her family first moved to New England. The excitement of all those free gifts, the refrigerator magnets, pot holders, key chains with can openers; the sponge that looked like a flat piece of cardboard until you dropped it in water to watch it expand into a lobster.

Maybe a batch of her famous triple chocolate brownies. No, that would be too much sugar for young children. Chocolate chip oatmeal cookies? Mixing dough in the kitchen, Emma anticipates the smell of baking.

So many years since she last did so. If she turned around, she could almost see Diana licking the beaters. Emma knows she shouldn't, not with her recently diagnosed diabetes, but she can't resist. She eats one of those gooey warm cookies straight from the oven. She'd forgotten the guilty pleasure.

Later, after she's wrapped the cookies, carried them to the cottage door and rung the bell, a moment of panic arrives. Listening for the sounds of life within, footsteps coming to the door,

Emma has a vision of herself, a total stranger, offering a plate of cookies on a paper plate. What would she say?

Hello, I'm Emma Nolan. I live next door. I saw your little girls from the bedroom window ...

No, you couldn't say that, not today. People would think you're a pedophile.

It's the mother who answers the door. Emma can see her unease as she contemplates the proffered plate. Emma wonders if she looks like a crackpot, a person who would bake a batch of poison cookies and deliver them to a family.

Waiting on the cottage porch, holding her foil-wrapped offering, Emma reconsiders her plan, but then the vacationing mother reaches out to take the plate from Emma's hands. "Oh," she says. "How wonderful. Would you like to come in?"

"Oh, no! No, thank you. I won't stay. I hope you don't think it's strange. Bringing over cookies this way. I live next door, and I love to bake. I used to have a little baking business in town. I shouldn't eat sweets. I thought perhaps the little girls ..." Her voice drifts away. "Enjoy your time in Belle Harbor," Emma adds, already heading to the buffer of the rose hedge.

"Thank you," the mother calls after her. "I'm sure we will."

When Diana calls from India that Sunday, Emma is happy for once to have news to share. Happy news.

"Guess what? I dusted off my baking sheets. You don't know how lovely it is to smell cookies in the house again. It reminds me of when you and your brother were small."

"Mom," her daughter replies, "why are you baking? You have diabetes."

"I brought cookies to the renters next door."

"You brought cookies to renters. Why would you do that?"

"It's just an idea I had. So I did it."

"Are you all right, Mom? I mean tell me honestly."

"Of course I'm all right." The question annoys Emma. "I haven't told you that the cottage changes hands every week now."

Emma also hasn't told her daughter that Maureen O'Malley died over the winter. If she doesn't speak those words, they're somehow less real. And what would Diana offer in return if she told her? What comfort could she bring from eight thousand miles away.

"I found myself watching each new wave of renters from the upstairs window," she says, "from Kyle's old room. People are so interesting, Diana. They really are. A new drama every week."

"Mom—wait—you're staring out the window like a Peeping Tom?"

"I'm not a Peeping Tom."

"Do you want to get a call from the police?"

"For giving people cookies?"

"Mom—" Diana's husband interjects. They must have her on speakerphone. Darrel never calls her "Mom." This must be his serious voice, the executive tone. "I think you should think about what Diana is saying."

"I have," Emma replies.

For her son-in-law to call her "Mom" in his commanding way seems more like an insult than an intimacy.

"I'll phone you next week," Emma tells them. And then she can't resist. "Unless someone shows up to arrest me."

The next guests are loud but Emma bakes them a plate of cookies anyway. After they depart a few days later, she's awakened in the middle of the night by raccoons foraging in the trash. Emma hears their chattering shrieks from her bedroom and looks outside to see two raccoons swinging from the bird feeder, the one Kyle built long ago.

The next morning, if she'd had a gun, she would have killed those beasts once she discovered the shattered pieces, the feed tray gnawed by ratty little teeth. Emma, who wouldn't even kill a spider, who captures them to set free, imagines getting a pellet gun to shoot those greedy indifferent foragers, to pick them off one by one from her porch. Of course she never would. The fantasy keeps her from crying.

Gathering the wrecked fragments of her son's feeder, Emma wraps them in one of Kyle's old Red Sox T-shirts, and pushes it to the back of her sock drawer. Let Diana and her husband figure that one out after she's gone! In its dismembered state, she doubts Diana would recognize the bird feeder, the gift her brother built one Mother's Day. She might not recognize the remnants of her brother's ratty old Sox T-shirt either. Emma pictures them finding it, shaking their heads, asking each other, "Mom, what the—?"

Assuming they even take the time to contemplate what she leaves behind. A more likely scenario, Emma knows, is that they'll just toss her possessions without a thought. A dumpster parked on the lawn, the accumulated treasures and trash of a lifetime chucked out without lingering, as quickly as possible, so they can jet back to their lives.

She cleans up the field of food wrappers and soda cans scattered over both yards. The red paper plate that had held her cookies blows across her vision along with an Oreos wrapper. In that moment, Emma decides maybe Diana is right, though not for her reasons. What was she thinking, making cookies for strangers?

An older couple without children rent the cottage toward the end of summer. They remind Emma of herself and her husband long ago. The nostalgic memory is ruined midweek when the vacationing couple erupt into a screaming argument out on the deck. Emma shuts the kitchen window against the sound. It gives her goosebumps to hear their voices.

Emma and Jim would never have yelled at each other like that. Emma can recall few legitimate arguments, although they had rocky times in the course of forty years of marriage. That was true of all long-married couples.

Divorce was out of the question in their day. Not that they ever contemplated divorce, but sometimes Emma thinks that maybe she never really knew Jim. Could that be true? Could you be married to a man for more than forty years and in the end, you never really knew each other?

Her life had been happy enough back then, the children, her garden, her friends, Jim with his work. People didn't question things like young people do now. Diana and her husband were always off to couples retreats, marriage "encounters." Before they moved to India, her daughter and her husband belonged to one of those charismatic churches where marriage was worshipped like a god. They took her to a service once. Emma wanted to run as soon as they pulled into the parking lot. So many bumper stickers, so many earnest couples.

When the police come to the cottage that night, Emma is awakened by the squawk of a patrol car radio in the driveway. Her silly joke to Diana returns, before she realizes the police are there for the people next door, the arguing older couple in the cottage. For a moment, Emma lies frozen in fear, straining to hear what is being said. In the morning, she checks the town paper's police notes: *Domestic dispute on Fairview Road. No arrests were made.*

The couple pack up and leave before noon, but the cops drive by slowly several times that afternoon, peering at Emma's house as well as the rental, as though she, too, were implicated in the fight the night before. The creepy cop, the one she never liked, dating back to when her children were teenagers. Sergeant Rusty would hide in trees, dropping down like a monkey to scatter a party of teens. The kids nicknamed him Curious George for his receding hairline and dopey grin.

As always, summer ends too soon. A storm blows in without warning one afternoon at the end of August. Dark clouds build over the ocean; the wind overturns the umbrella on the deck next door and tumbles it across the yard. The branches of the giant willow dance in the breeze. Little boys come down the street, bicycling in formation, furiously pedaling home ahead of the approaching thunderstorm. Emma stands at her bedroom window, suddenly afraid. The light is greenish yellow; a summer afternoon like this seems a window out of time.

The summer he turned eighteen, Kyle slipped through the crack.

He died while waterskiing. A speeding daredevil at the wheel, a name she'd never heard before, a group of summer people he'd met at the quarry. A teenager racing a speedboat too fast across Vernon Lake. Her son died immediately, the doctors later said. A blow to the head. Jim was away on business.

Emma drove to the hospital in New Vernon alone. It was a Saturday night, the emergency room brimming with accidents, overdoses, crying children. A fisherman with a hand wrapped in a bloody T-shirt sat by himself in the corner. He was still wearing tall boots, slick with brine. Emma would always wonder why she noticed the vividness of those green boots, before someone ushered her into a room behind a closed curtain.

Later, she sat in the security office as a burly guard methodically checked off the contents of her son's pockets, items retrieved one by one from a brown envelope then laid on the desk as the officer described them. He was a tough man, but not without compassion. One cigarette lighter. That was a surprise—did Kyle smoke? The silly good luck charm he always carried attached to his keys; a ridiculously small amount of money, a few bills and thirty-seven cents. She stared at those three dimes, two pennies, a nickel, as though meaning might be found there.

Back at home, sitting down alone at the kitchen table, she forced herself to look through the rest of her son's wallet. A black-and-white photo in the billfold, the two of them at the lake, the summer he turned eight. A battered foil-wrapped condom tucked in a side pocket. Did he ever have the chance to use one?

The next day, she went to get his old car from where he'd parked at the quarry. The tape player sprung to life with the ignition, the last song Kyle heard blasting through the car. *Let's Hang On!* On the bumpy dirt road back to town, her son's heavy good luck key chain swung in time to the Four Seasons, a pendulum keeping time against her knees.

They were always close. Jim away so often. Emma used to wonder if a boy that close to his mother would grow up to be gay. That wouldn't have bothered her. What she feared was his life turning out more difficult than it had to be. Who cared about such things anymore, but back then it seemed a big deal. To think she spent even an hour wondering how life would turn out for her son if he were gay, when what really happened was that Kyle never reached manhood at all.

Emma had returned home to an empty house on a day much like this one, the end of summer, the season fading. The angle of light is already sharper in the afternoons, a coolness in the air. It's only four in the afternoon, a storm approaching, but the steep light tells her the sun has already begun its descent. Summer is ending.

She thinks of something she should have done a long time ago.

Kyle's keys with their futile good luck charm, the knell against her knees, are still in her jewelry box. She's kept them all these years.

She unlocks the box, cradling her son's key chain in her palm. Emma cannot bear the thought of this last remnant of her son—an object he touched in his last hours on earth—winding up in the dumpster with everything else.

Kneeling at the edge of the front garden, Emma finds a spot below their cat's favorite lilac bush. She digs a hole in the earth and buries her son's keys in the ground.

CHAPTER 5

The Cradle

IN HER HEART, she knew the baby was a boy. In her third month, Catharine stepped into the spring air from the little bookstore on the harbor, and a cramp doubled her over, forcing her to clutch a nearby bench for balance. When the pain passed, she hurried to the nearest restroom, at Town Beach. The heavy steel door clanged behind her like a prison gate. The familiar "Shower At Your Own Risk" sign, which always seemed like a joke in the past, now spelled a warning.

In the stall, she found a clump of blood that looked like a Rorschach clot. Another cramp arrived, piercing until it passed. Catharine stared at the bloody tissue in her hands. A shape that resembled a piece of smashed fruit that should have been a baby.

Was she supposed to just flush it down the toilet?

She couldn't bring herself to do that. This baby had wanted to be born. She'd felt his spirit strongly. A boy. She'd already pictured him. Tom's eyes, her smile. She let the heavy door slam behind her. She took the ramp down to the beach. No one was watching.

Catharine took off her sandals and left them on the sand. She waded out into the cold Atlantic, swirled her hand into the current and, after a few waves, let the tissue go, watching it melt into sea. A song unspooled in her head. *Bye, bye, baby. Baby, goodbye.*

Why did so many old songs have those lyrics? They echoed in her head as she ran to her car, clutching her middle against another cramp, crying so no one could hear. Tom held her in his arms when he found her on the porch, standing before the door, tears down her cheeks. "What happened? Are you hurt?"

"I didn't want to tell you."

"Tell me what? Cat, what happened?"

"I was pregnant again."

Tom had a plan he announced once she was up and feeling better. "I think I'm going to build a cradle," he said at breakfast one morning. "I think that's what we need. A beautiful, hand-crafted, wooden cradle. A talisman for the future."

Catharine couldn't think of anything more heartbreaking. Or less likely. "You don't have the tools," she said.

"I'll find tools."

"Have you ever built anything before?"

"Don't be negative. Please." He held both her hands in his. "I'm trying to see our way into something better. It's school vacation next week. This is something I can do. I can do this for us, Catharine."

"Okay," she agreed. "If that's what you need to do. Build a cradle. Just do it in the basement. I don't want to have to look at it."

She refused to go down there to check on him, but she knew he was working by the frantic sounds of saws and hammering. After a few days without sleep, Tom wandered the house in his bathrobe, unshaven, his hair carefully combed. He was always vain about his hair, his ragged Sam Shepard looks.

It was a half a day before Catharine realized Tom wasn't in the basement working. He was gone. She phoned the department chairman, Tom's faculty friends. Though she couldn't imagine why he'd be there, she even tried Tom's mother. She waited until after midnight, and then she started phoning hospitals. The next morning, she dialed the police. Listening to the ringing phone, waiting for each call to be answered, Catharine felt her panic rising. But also something terrifying, a small, trapped voice inside hoping to be free.

That night, Tom finally phoned. He'd checked himself into McLean, the psychiatric hospital where his parents had him briefly committed after his first breakdown, the one in prep school which she only learned about years later.

When he was a sophomore, Tom fled campus just before Christmas and broke into a beach motel that was closed for the season. He holed up there for a week before his parents found him. That was the first time his father had to pull strings to make Tom's transgressions go away.

Now, he'd driven their ten-year-old Volkswagen an hour or more to the hospital in Belmont. The psychiatrist he'd recently started seeing agreed to sign him in. Catharine couldn't believe he hadn't hit another car or killed himself driving that distance on the highway. She took the train into Boston, two buses and a cab, to find Tom reading the newspaper in the corner of an airy, unlocked ward.

He looked disheveled, but no worse, really, than the day she came home sobbing and he held her in his arms on the porch, no worse than the morning he'd descended into the basement to build a cradle. He wore a hospital johnny and a cotton bathrobe tied at the waist, white terry cloth slippers. He hadn't shaved in days. He looked up and smiled when he saw her.

"James Taylor wrote a song here," he said by way of greeting.

"Did he really?"

"You know what else?" Tom asked in a bright tone. He seemed like a small boy. She was relieved to hear him laugh. "Robert Lowell lived just down the hall when he was a patient." In a dramatic voice Tom added, "Over in the locked ward."

Catharine bent to kiss his cheek and took a seat beside him. "The friendly ghost of Robert Lowell."

Across the room, a man hunched over a jigsaw puzzle by the window suddenly swept his arm across the pieces and overturned the table. Two male nurses hurried to his side.

"So what happened, Tom?" she forced herself to ask when it seemed he'd drifted back into his thoughts.

"I don't know." He shook his head.

"You just took off?"

Tom rolled his shoulders and looked out the window. "I should have told you."

"Do you think?"

He turned to her with panicked eyes. "Build a fucking cradle! Who am I kidding? The wood looks like a five-year-old took a hammer to it. It's a piece of junk."

"No, it's not."

"Have you seen it?"

Catharine had descended into the basement to look for Tom two nights before, but she hadn't noticed the cradle. She shook her head.

"Trust me." He rubbed his temples and shut his eyes. "It's ridiculous."

"Tom." Catharine spoke quietly.

"My father was right."

"Don't say that. Come on, what good does it do to go there?" Catharine laid her hand on his knee. "Don't bring your father into this, Tom-Tom."

Tom looked startled. "What did you call me?"

"Tom-Tom. I don't know where that came from."

"My mother used to call me that."

"Not the voice I was aiming for."

Tom laughed. "You sounded affectionate. My mother when I was a child, not the bitch she is now." He searched her eyes. "You and I haven't spoken to each other with affection since— maybe before London."

"I'm sure we have," she said. "Expressed affection."

"Cat-woman," Tom whispered, leaning over to kiss her neck. Despite everything, he still radiated his old magnetism. "What have you done with my aggrieved wife?"

He moved his chair closer. She saw clarity in his eyes, not the jagged hurt of before, the spirit of his father's disapproval hovering in the room.

"Tom," Catharine said. "Why can't you always be this way? Funny, charming. Your real self. The man you are right now, not the—"

Not what? Catharine searched for a word, her eyes circling the room.

"Not my illness?" Tom asked. "Do you know how much I wish I could? Be that person you want me to be."

"I know, Tom."

"I don't know where he goes," he said, "but when happy Tom leaves, I'm in darkness."

She retrieved the car keys from his possessions in the nurse's station. In the parking lot, Catharine found their old blue Beetle abandoned at an angle between two spaces as though he'd pulled into a space after a long drive and had to bolt. She was surprised it hadn't been towed. When she unlocked the driver's door, she inhaled the smell of a rancid cheeseburger and melted iced coffee. The Sunday *Times* was scattered in sections over the passenger floor. French fries, a change of clothes, his running shoes, a pad of scribbled paper, colored pens.

She turned the ignition and the radio blasted NPR, which was so like Tom. Lose track of reality but keep up with the news. She laid her head on the steering wheel and, for the first time since he wandered away, allowed herself to cry.

That night, she looked in the basement. The pieces of wood Tom had hammered together to resemble a cradle lay on their side, as though he'd kicked them over. Tools and wood shavings were strewn across the floor. A crumbled piece of three-ring paper held the crude design he'd drawn in red Sharpie, the same bold strokes he'd used to outline his communal arts center plans years before.

She put away the tools, swept the floor, wrapped the semblance of a cradle and Tom's sketch in an old sheet. She hauled the bundle up three flights of stairs to a far corner of the attic, and hoped he'd never ask where it was, and he didn't.

CHAPTER 6

Unto Us

CATHARINE STOOD in the hallway outside Tom's study. He was on new meds; the doctor seemed hopeful. He was hunched over his desk. Catharine watched him in silence. The architect's lamp above his head bathed him in its glow. From a distance, it looked as though he were writing in one of his old notebooks, the ones he loved.

"Are you writing?" Catharine asked, and immediately wished she hadn't.

Tom shut the notebook and turned around. "It's nothing."

"You don't know that."

He tossed the pen onto his desk and got to his feet. She saw he was still in the bathrobe he'd worn all day.

"Tom—" She reached for his arm as he headed for the door. "I'm sorry. I shouldn't have asked."

"Oh Catharine," he whispered. "Why am I always the one making you sorry?"

All those childless years she could have left, and yet Catharine stayed married to Tom. Partly it was the memory of how she'd loved him when they were young. Somehow she always would.

Catharine feared what might happen to them both if she ever did leave. The truth, she finally decided, must be that she wasn't that unhappy in the end. She couldn't imagine leaving this place. Without Tom, she couldn't imagine staying. From the first day she'd viewed the house on Fairview Road, Catharine knew she had to live in Belle Harbor, the place she'd been searching for all her life.

Tom didn't really hope for a family after McLean. The universe had rendered its judgment. Tom was proud of his resigned acceptance. To remain childless was the way life had happened to them, that was all. It would only make things worse to dwell on it. He was resigned and she should be, too.

Her husband was resigned about everything. That was the problem. Catharine liked to joke that Tom had taken early retirement.

From his job? people asked.

No. From life.

Her friends at school admired her sense of humor. You're so funny! They seldom knew when she was serious.

In her attic room, Catharine forced herself to release her grief into writing. A poem a day, as she'd once poured herself into journals. She wrote about Tom, his disappearance into himself. Where did he go? Why was it never better when he returned? She wrote about losing her beloved cousin Buddy whom she still grieved, years after his Navy helicopter crash. She described all she felt in nature, the wisdom of the stars at night from her window, the moods of the sea, the passage of time.

Usually she tore up what she wrote. Sometimes she didn't. She never sent work out to be published. And then one day Catharine came upon the poem she'd written years ago, "Emma's Kitchen," and she gathered it with her new work to enter a small press contest and her manuscript, *Fearful Symmetry*, won. The judge compared her voice to Mary Oliver's.

"You won?"

She'd hesitated to tell Tom, fearing he might view her achievement as one more failing on his part, but he seemed genuinely pleased by the news.

"You don't have to sound that surprised," Catharine said with a laugh.

"No. My God. You deserve it. You're amazing, Cat." He bounded across the room to lift her in his arms. "Let's celebrate. How shall we celebrate?"

"Let's get a bottle of champagne."

"Champagne?"

"Or chardonnay," she added, ever mindful of their savings.

"No, champagne!" Tom decided. "For here, or shall we go out somewhere?"

"Let's go somewhere."

"Where?"

"Let's drive to Boston! Go back to Cambridge. Let's get a bottle of champagne and visit our old lives."

Tom said nothing for a time. "Our old lives. That doesn't sound like much of a celebration."

She met his expression and instantly grasped how absurd the idea was. Drive to Boston? It was nine o'clock; they both had to teach in the morning. And he was right. What kind of a night would it be to revisit the places they first met, fell in love, where their lives unraveled.

Tom stifled a yawn. She remembered he'd caught the early train, he'd been up since five. "We should just go to bed," she said, "have an early night for once. Catch up on rest. That would be a celebration."

"Or we could go to bed," Tom repeated, taking her by the shoulders. "Cat." He spoke into her eyes. For a while, they stood staring at each other. "Let's try again." His hands slid down her arms, circling her waist. "I think we've been afraid of it happening again," Tom said after a long silence. "Another miscarriage. It's too hard." Neither of them had acknowledged it, but months had passed since they last slept together.

"Why do we let ourselves drift so far apart?" Catharine asked.

"We're afraid," Tom said.

She held his face in her hands.

"It could be we'd be terrible parents," he said.

"I don't think so."

"I wish I had your faith."

"You didn't have an altar boy for a father."

After a while, he pulled her close. Catharine rested her head on his chest.

"Let's try," she said. "Third time's the charm."

Oh, the neediness, the sheer vulnerability of that fragile, rosy-faced package the nurse placed into Tom's arms the night Toby was born.

"You have a son, Mr. Osborne."

"God help me," he murmured.

"Yes, He will!" the nurse answered. She was compact and round, cheeks shining with joy, a tiny gold crucifix gleaming at her throat, a maternity nurse who clearly loved her job. "You show that little boy to your wife. She's waiting to see him."

"Oh my God, he's perfect," Catharine sobbed. "Tom, he's perfect."

"That was you," he said.

"No, no. You! Both of us. We made a perfect boy." Tom hoisted the tiny, swaddled package in his arms, and danced around the room, humming a verse from Handel's *Messiah*, then singing it aloud in his booming dramatic voice: *"For unto us—a child is born! Unto us—a son is given ... and his name shall be called—"* He stopped singing and looked at her quizzically. He took a seat beside her on the bed. "What were we going to call him?"

"We talked about this, didn't we?" Catharine was giddy with exhaustion. "I know we did. My brain is mush." Here was the son who'd been trying to be born all those years. She felt him alive in her arms. "Toby. We said we'd call him Toby."

"Toby. Yes! Toby's not a name, though, is it?" Tom asked. "He needs a full name. Didn't we have one?"

"Tobias?" Catharine shook her head. "No, that's not it." Strands of hair lay plastered to her forehead in sweat.

"You know right now?" Tom said. "You look more beautiful than I've ever seen you."

In his gaze, Catharine saw herself as he did, her face twisted, blotchy from effort, ecstatic. Catharine touched his cheek. "Not Tobias."

"Toblerone?" Tom tried. "'A loaf of bread, a jug of wine, a Toblerone bar. And thou.'" He always loved when he could make her laugh. "How many of those did we eat? That train ride to Madrid. What year was that?"

"'83?"

"You can't name a child Toblerone."

"We'd never have to call him that. We'd call him Toby. The longer version's just for—"

"—first day of class? high school graduation?" Catharine sat up straight against the pillows. "Imagine an auditorium where Toblerone Osborne is called to the stage. Our son will hate us."

Tom leaned across the bed. He kissed her forehead. "Who cares about school? He's our child. We get to name him whatever we want."

Catharine peeked inside the blue receiving blanket at the newborn old man's face. "Are you our Toby?" The baby lifted a little fist, then clasped her outstretched finger.

"Tobin?" Tom offered. "Like the bridge to Boston."

"A bridge?" Catharine thought about it. "Yes. A bridge!"

Tom bent to kiss his son's head. "Hello Toby," he said.

Catharine closed her eyes. People arrived on earth lugging such baggage from the past, their parents, their parents' parents, who knew what you were still carrying, what sins of the fathers, sins of the mothers, you could be working out. She vowed then that their child, their long-awaited child would be happy. As she herself had seldom been, as Tom never was.

"We were lucky," Tom said.

Catharine tried to joke. "How unlike us!" She laughed. "To be lucky."

CHAPTER 7

Dance, Then

TOM'S FACE WAS FLUSHED as he spun past with Toby on his shoulders, the two of them madly hurtling through the matinee crowd of Christmas revelers in Sanders Theatre. They'd started the celebratory dance through the lobby together, their little family, seven-year-old Toby holding his parents' hands as they joined the Revels cast pouring off the stage for the long, snaking parade that marked intermission.

Parallel ropes of dancers wove tightly together as the orchestra and mezzanine emptied and then the balcony, a theater full of swirling bodies piling into the cavernous lobby to join the dance. The actors with their strong voices echoing through the hall, their faces theatrical in pancake makeup and kohl eyes; the crowd pressing closer, ever closer, before the frenzied rush of dancers swept Catharine into another line.

Toby was laughing, perched upon his father's shoulders as Catharine watched them carried away by the crowd. Tom seemed more alive than she'd seen him in months, bellowing with gusto: *Dance, then, wherever you may be! I am the*

Lord of the Dance, said he! Tom grinned at her each time they bounded past in their opposite lines, his eyes shining. She hoped he was okay.

As a freshman at Harvard, Tom had once plunged from the balcony of this theater down to a mezzanine row below. The first time he told her the story, he described it as an accident. He was high, he said, making his way along the wide upper-tier railing like a tightrope walker, when he lost his balance and plummeted fifteen feet to the seats below. He'd fractured a leg and three ribs; he'd sprained a wrist.

The second time she heard the story, it had a different ending, but by then they were already married. It was the statues that did it, Tom confessed. The Sanders Theatre statues urging him on. He'd never intended to harm himself that day, unhappy as he'd been. He never meant to kill himself as people later said. Those immortal statues flanking the stage urged him to jump, gazing in judgment at his failures, with their tapered marble hands, proud chins, icy unseeing eyes.

Tom had just broken up with a girl, but that wasn't the reason he impulsively vaulted from the balcony on an ordinary morning after a history class. He didn't know why he did it, beyond the static screaming in his head. The statues had not been indifferent. They wanted him to jump.

He'd landed banged up but half upright on a wooden mezzanine bench, as though he'd stumbled finding a seat. Not much of a calamity in the end. He wasn't suicidal, his parents insisted to each other and anyone who'd heard the news of Tom's fall.

Father and son had a different conversation. "I trust you weren't trying to kill yourself," is what Noah Osborne said. "I'd hate to think you even failed at that."

"Oh my God," Catharine gasped when Tom eventually told her this. "He didn't really say that?"

"He did."

It brought her to tears to think anyone could say those words to their own child. "Your father is a monster."

"Now you understand," Tom said.

Catharine watched her little son balanced on her husband's shoulders as they whirled past in the lobby once more. She hoped Tom wouldn't drop him. Rays of sun filtered through the stained glass windows in the stairwell, assuring her he wouldn't. Tom was on new medication, which seemed to be working.

Her son clung to his father's strong shoulders with his little legs, both fists wrapped around Tom's neck. He didn't look afraid. He looked triumphant, laughing and singing along with the chorus. Toby was getting so tall. How much longer would he be the boy carried aloft this way? Catharine wondered if this might be the last year.

Watching mothers with babies when she was a teenager, Catharine always thought she would hate motherhood. Being consumed like that. The overwhelming need, the sheer messiness of spit-up and diapers, little hands entangled in your hair, tugging and twisting, mouths sucking on your flesh. It was bliss. She loved watching her son nurse as an infant, his hunger and need, his gratitude expressed in tiny hands stroking her breast.

The actor playing the Lord of the Dance thundered past. *Dance! Dance! Wherever you may be!* he sang in his magnificent baritone, and Catharine briefly locked eyes with him, resplendent in velvet and gold. He waved his white handkerchief high, the bells of the Morris men jingling behind him.

St. George slew the dragon, but even he must die. To be born again! Catharine loved that Revels scene each year, the solemn Morris men's sword dance that preceded intermission, but it also left her confused. Why didn't he fight harder to live? Why must he die?

In a moment, the music would end, the dancing stop, and a cheer rise up from the crowd before its energy collapsed like a balloon, people wandering off to find chocolate and bathrooms and drinks. Catharine had lost track of Tom and Toby in the crush of bodies.

They would be all right. Of course they would. Tom would gently lower Toby to the ground and firmly hold his hand in the press of jubilant revelers. He'd buy him a small bag of cookies or a brownie and make Toby promise to save half for the long ride home. He was a good father. Catharine knew this.

Toby was breathless, rosy-cheeked, when she finally found them where she knew they would be, hovering by the refreshment stand. Toby was fine. He would always be fine. Her talisman against all harm. Toby would never inherit the family disease.

"Did you see us?" Toby gushed. "Dad was awesome! He had me on his shoulders the whole time!"

"I saw." Catharine tousled her son's hair. "Did you spot me? I was dancing, too."

Toby shook his head.

Catharine got down on one knee and looked at him intently. "Toby, tell me really, was that fun?"

"That was so much fun!" he exclaimed. "Can we do that again?"

"Next year."

Toby groaned. "We have to wait a whole year?"

Catharine kissed the top of her son's forehead and got to her feet. "We'll practice at home."

"But it won't be the same."

"Even if Dad carries you on his shoulders?"

Catharine glanced up at Tom. He was looking down at her, his expression hopeful, wary, craving something. His eyes glowed in that eager way she associated with his manic periods. She tried to erase the thought, to unsee what she'd glimpsed in his face, but she couldn't.

He leaned forward and circled an arm around her waist, pulling her close. "You don't have to worry about me anymore, Cat," he whispered.

"I know," she lied.

CHAPTER 8

Happily Ever After

WHEN THE COTTAGE NEXT DOOR went on the market, Catharine hoped whoever bought it this time would actually live there, that they'd have quiet neighbors, maybe another family with a young boy Toby's age. A couple from New York had used it as a summer place in recent years. Catharine was scarcely aware when they were there.

Her school vacation had just begun the June morning she heard the first car pulling into the driveway next door, followed by a second. Slamming doors, raised voices punctured the lovely silence where she sat in her third-floor refuge, gazing at the sky and a ribbon of ocean below, rewording the line of a poem.

She knew the cottage had been sold to a couple from Germany that spring. They'd come for a week early in April. They hadn't told Catharine the place was to once more become a summer rental.

"It's smaller than it looked in the photo," a woman's voice called from the driveway. "Don't start," a man answered. "It's only for a week."

Catharine closed the window above the cottage. It wasn't hot yet but it would be soon.

In summer, Tom spent most days in his basement darkroom. He'd bought himself a used camera for the new millennium and it turned out he had a good eye for architecture, nature scenes, views from the train window on his way to teach in the city. He captured strangers frozen in time on the Orange Line platform in Sullivan Square as they flew by his subway window, random scenes on the street.

He seldom wrote anymore. Once she'd opened one of his notebooks and quickly closed it. It was the notebook he always kept on his desk, as though he were still writing. The last entry was dated five years before. "All my words are gone," it read.

The fact that Tom had lost his gift made her uneasy about her own work, as though her intention had been to wound him, to steal Tom's brilliance, when really she'd begun with no intention at all, a spontaneous act of grief. He never talked about poetry anymore, though he encouraged her.

Catharine never showed him a word. Her writing no longer seemed something to share. She rarely sent work out to be published. She wasn't sure why beyond a flickering sense of guilt, as though she'd taken it from Tom.

The arrival of those first weekly renters was the prelude of more to come, the summer people, the soundtrack next door breaking into her thoughts as she stared into space, pen in hand, watching the changing light.

The Europeans, sunbathing nude on the deck, as though they were on a beach in France and not in a neighborhood. Ten-year-old Toby was amazed. He ran up the attic stairs, shouting: "Mom! Mom! Look out the window."

Catharine rose from her desk unsure what she was about to see. She burst out laughing and Toby ran to the window and joined her.

Two young couples with children rented the following week. Catharine heard them in the driveway, smoking cigarettes, drinking beers after the kids were in bed. Despite herself, she stopped to listen to their dual dialogue, the men talking about bands they'd seen, the women about their children.

"You have that album?"

"Oh, man, that album must be worth—? You should totally sell that album."

"Doesn't lithium make you kill yourself?" one of the women asked the other, and Catharine was brought back with a jolt to her life. Tom was on lithium. He had been for years.

That first year set the pattern, a cacophonous weekly turnover of summer renters: volleyball on the lawn, beach towels strung across the deck, bicycles abandoned where they fell, brightly colored boogie boards stacked against the house like tribal shields, cars parked at strange angles across the front lawn. Cigarette smoke wafted from the driveway, laughter pealing from the deck until, at last, it was Labor Day, the end of the weekly turmoil, if only for a few months. The last renters of the season.

They were a honeymoon couple, remnants of shaving cream congratulations still faintly visible on the window of their sports car. The late afternoon light was already changing, a hint of fall in the evening air. Catharine watched from her window as they exchanged kisses, idly spinning in circles on the long ropes of the towering willow's wooden swing.

Making dinner in the kitchen, Catharine saw them playing softball on the lawn, their voices drifting through the open window.

"Come on, you have to throw better than that," the man admonished his new bride. "Why would I know how to do that?" She laughed.

Catharine overheard the husband keeping score. "I'm still ahead!"

"It feels like a bit of a letdown, doesn't it?" The woman distractedly pitched another ball which bounced on the ground before the groom whacked it with his bat.

"What does?"

"The wedding! You look forward to something all those months, and then it's over."

Catharine waited for an answer but didn't hear one.

When she pulled into her driveway at the same time as her neighbors a few days later, the woman lingered by her car. "Hi!" She waved. "I've seen you up there, working in your window."

Catharine smiled to think that the people next door had been watching her, too.

"Are you a writer?" the woman continued.

"I write poetry." Catharine paused. "In the summer, I write poetry. The rest of the time, I'm a teacher."

"What do you teach?"

"Middle school art."

"I love art. And poetry!" the girl said. She seemed like a girl to Catharine, her cheeks shining like a teenager's. "I'd like to read some."

"My poems?"

"I would. And I need something to read. I forgot my book."

"You're on your honeymoon, right?"

"Oh." The woman laughed. "I didn't realize it was that obvious. We were married last Sunday. My folks gave us a week in Belle Harbor. We used to come here as kids. My grandmother actually owned this cottage years ago."

"Your grandmother was Maureen O'Malley?"

"Did you know her?"

"No, I wish I had. I've heard the neighborhood stories."

"Nana and the woman who owned your place were great friends. They had a lot of fun together in the summers." The young woman looked back at the little cottage. "I have such wonderful memories of Belle Harbor. I've always loved it here. The light."

"Me, too."

"Listen," the girl said, "I'm serious. I'd love to read your poetry."

Catharine hesitated.

"I would."

"On your honeymoon?"

"I was an English major!" The girl smiled.

"Okay, sure," Catharine said at last. "Let me go hunt up a copy."

"Can I pay you?"

"What? No, it's a gift."

The woman was waiting, leaning against her car door when Catharine returned with a copy of *Fearful Symmetry*.

"I love your garden, by the way," she said.

"Thanks. Don't look at the weeds."

"You have to sign it!" the girl insisted, pushing the slim volume back into Catharine's hands. A pen was produced from her purse. Catharine tried to think of what to inscribe to this young woman embarking on a life. She had no advice. Only hope.

"Happily Ever After!" she finally scribbled above her signature and the date. September 7, 2001.

The next day, they were gone, returned to their lives in the city.

The delightful young couple. As she and Tom had once been.

As she always did, Catharine rejoiced at the prospect of September, though it meant the end of school vacation and a return to her job and no free time. The weekend after Labor Day, the cottage was closed, water turned off for winter, the deck's sprawling summer gear gone from view. Adirondack chairs stacked beneath the deck, umbrella and lurking black-covered grill taken inside, the end of the sound and spectacle of renters until spring. She could finally look out her window and see peace.

No way of knowing then how fleeting peace would be.

Tom was flying to L.A. that second week of September. He seldom attended academic conferences, but his department friend Syd Rosen convinced him they should go to this one. Catharine was glad for him to have the chance to get away. For

Tom to step outside himself for a week, and she was happy for herself, to be alone.

She dropped him at the airport for his flight to L.A., and turned up the radio once she got back on the highway. Tom had been listening to NPR on the drive down, but she'd lowered the volume to concentrate on the zigzag of Boston traffic angling through Logan.

American Flight 11 had crashed into the World Trade Center in New York minutes before. She would always remember her first thought: what an unbelievable accident. She didn't yet know it was a flight to L.A. A few exits down the highway, the radio reported United Flight 175 had done the same. Catharine's heart froze. That plane, too, was flying to L.A. from Boston. As was Tom.

Her mind went blank. American? United? She couldn't remember what airline Tom was flying. How many Boston to L.A. flights would there be in the same hour of the morning?

She'd dropped him into the curbside frenzy of triple-parked cars, rental car buses, hotel vans, the silver tips of planes gliding past far out on the tarmac. She leaned across the front seat and patted Tom's knee. "Knock 'em dead." He grabbed his bag from the back seat and was gone. Did she kiss his cheek? She wasn't sure.

And in that moment, imagining Tom gone, in a way that was beyond imagining, all the weight they carried between them across the years, the disappointments, resentments, none of it mattered anymore.

"Come back," she prayed.

She sped the rest of the way home, ran up the stairs to his study, searching for some clue as to what flight he was on, but he'd taken his laptop. She went through the papers on his desk, his wastebasket, held up his white notepad to the light to see if it bore the imprint of a note he'd jotted down. The college had booked the tickets. She dialed his cell phone which went straight to voicemail. Every few minutes she dialed it again.

Toby's school was dismissed early, and Catharine was relieved that he'd be home and she wouldn't be alone. She drove the short distance to pick him up, queuing in a long line of stunned parents waiting at the curb.

He looked stricken when he got into the car.

"Do you think Dad's dead?" he asked once he shut the door.

"No." Catharine was firm. "No, I'd know." She thought that was true, a genuine feeling as she'd once sensed the spirits of children. Or was that fooling herself? Unwilling to face what that would mean if Tom was on one of those planes.

"I don't think so. We have to believe that." Catharine wondered if her voice sounded as uncertain to Toby as it did to her ear.

"Is this the end of the world?"

Toby had always seemed so responsible for his age, sometimes Catharine forgot he was only ten years old. She reached across the front seat to put an arm around her son. "Say a prayer. Think of him safe somewhere, that he's okay."

He phoned late in the afternoon, almost evening.

"Oh my God, Tom," she sobbed into the phone.

"I love you," he said.

"I love you, too."

"Where are you?"

"Cleveland."

"Cleveland?"

"We had to land. All the flights are grounded. They kept us on the tarmac for two hours, then the FBI had to talk to people. Syd and I, we just got here. They're putting us up in a hotel."

"I was afraid it might have been your flight. I didn't think so, but I couldn't remember. I couldn't remember," she cried. "But, Tom, you're okay."

"We were on Delta. The college booked Delta. It was cheaper, Syd said. Of course they booked the cheaper flight."

"You're so lucky," Catharine sobbed. "We're so lucky."

"For the second time," Tom said. Catharine remembered he'd said that when Toby was born.

"Let's do better."

"We will," Tom promised. "We will."

That winter, the cottage was for sale again. The previous owners decided that given all that was happening in the world, they wouldn't be flying from Europe to the U.S. as often as they'd imagined. Catharine and Tom spent several fevered evenings scrambling to figure out how they could afford a down payment. If they bought the cottage, they could have some small control over who their summer neighbors would be.

Finally, Tom decided to do what he dreaded the most and ask his parents for the money. But before he could, another offer on the cottage was accepted. The couple from Germany, who'd once told Catharine they didn't like trees, sold to a landscape architect in Florida.

CHAPTER 9

People Next Door

THE CITY RENTERS HAD BEEN in the cottage a week when Toby encountered the boy on the bike path above the headlands. They were about the same age; Toby had turned twelve that summer. The boy rode a silver mountain bike, sleek and new. Toby had no idea how much a bike like that might cost. His was an old Schwinn his father brought home from the town swap shop. Together they'd fixed it up and that was fun. They worked on it every Saturday morning one spring. Weeknights his father was too tired to do anything but read after his long commute to the city, and often he fell asleep doing that. Toby's bike was special to him for that reason.

Toby's father taught English at a community college an hour away. "You're a saint!" he'd heard his parents' friends say, but his father always met that praise with a peculiar smile. His mother would laugh, though she didn't seem amused. Toby liked it best when only his mom or dad was home. The house changed when they were there together. Sometimes Toby wondered if that was his fault, and he wished he wasn't an only child. In a house filled with brothers and sisters, maybe his parents would have been happier.

Sitting in the back seat on their long Sunday drives into the country, Toby invented different lives for his mother and father as they rode in silence up front, the college music station fading in and out. His father was a secret, brilliant scientist; his mother a famous stage actress who preferred the quiet life of a seacoast town.

"Cool bike." The boy from the cottage flashed a sideways smile the morning they met on the trail. His name was Jake; he was wearing sunglasses attached to a neon green cord. Toby couldn't tell if he was mocking him.

"You're the one with the cool bike, man."

"Nah, this one's a rental." Jake adjusted the seat. "From the bike shop in town. You should see my wheels at home."

Toby wondered what else the family had rented. Did they rent the croquet set he'd watched them unbox on the wide lawn beyond the hedge? The huge tent the boy and his dad pitched next door on clear nights?

"Where are you headed?" the boy asked.

"Nowhere."

"Me too."

That was the start of their bond. Toby was slight, sandy-haired, and that summer had fallen into the habit of checking his face each morning for hints that the peachy down covering his cheeks would one day turn to whiskers. He couldn't help noticing Jake already had a faint shadow of those.

Through the early days of summer, when Jake wasn't busy with his family and their guests, the two boys rode their bikes into town for ice cream or an afternoon spent poking through comics at the antique store. Once or twice, Jake had come over to Toby's when the cottage's internet was slow, and they played old video games upstairs in Toby's room. Toby's mom made brownies one rainy afternoon and Jake said they were the best he'd ever tasted. "My mom never bakes."

Toby's mom laughed. "It's only a mix." Jake asked for the box top so he could show his mother what brand to buy, and Toby felt proud.

Late in July, when the weather turned brutally hot, Toby and Jake pedaled out to the quarry. That spring, Toby had joined the swim team at school. He loved the concentration of swimming, the sensation of being submerged in another world: the smell of chlorine on his skin, the sound of the coach's whistle heard underwater, the echo of the cheering crowd, the wrinkles on his fingers when he emerged from an hour in the pool, imagining himself a creature from the deep, an old man.

"That's just a pond." Jake shrugged at his first sight of the quarry from where they locked their bikes above the cliff. "I thought you said we were going to a rock quarry."

"It used to be a quarry. Like fifty years ago or something." Toby led the way down a steep slope to the swimming ledge. "When they stopped hauling granite, it filled with water. Guess how deep it is?"

"I don't know, twenty feet?"

"No, more. Guess."

"Fifty?"

Toby shook his head.

"I don't know," Jake said. "Just tell me."

"A hundred feet! Maybe more. It's so deep, if you sank— they'd never find your body."

Jake scoffed. "Divers would."

"I bet not. Divers have been down there before and never found what they were looking for. There really is a body down there. Trapped in a pickup truck."

"No way."

"It's true. It's like a town myth."

"If it's a myth, that means it's not true."

"Myths can be true."

"No, they can't."

"A legend then."

Jake thought about this for a second. "So, if there's really a body down there, why is nobody still looking?"

"Too cloudy. There's vegetation and stuff. You can't see the bottom."

Jake peered warily over the ledge as Toby flipped into the water and took a few quick backward strokes. "Come on! Let's swim."

Jake shook his head. "I don't know. I'm a little freaked out."

"Quarry Rules. You have to dive in. Or else you're a chicken."

Jake scanned the water, his arms wrapped around his chest. "I'm not a chicken."

"It's not that cold."

"I'm not afraid of the cold."

"What are you afraid of?"

"Nothing!" Jake dove from the rock then, though not a dive exactly, more a belly flop. He flailed his arms before treading water.

Toby dog-paddled closer. "You know how to swim, right?"

"Sure, I can swim," Jake said, but he didn't sound sure. "Just don't let me sink."

"Watch this!" Toby called and held his breath, plunging beneath the surface. He heard Jake calling his name, slowly at first, then with urgency.

When he resurfaced, Jake looked rattled. "Don't do that again, man."

By August, they were daring each other to swim the farthest, dive the deepest, to float beneath the cool green dark for as long as they could, eyes squeezed shut against whatever lurked there.

School was a few days away when Jake's family invited Toby for a sail on their boat before they returned to the city. Toby's mother was reworking a piece of writing at the old oak kitchen table. Once or twice, she'd published one of her poems somewhere, though Toby had the feeling she was always waiting for something more.

Toby stood in the kitchen doorway, watching her bent over her handwritten pages, her long braid tied with a ribbon. She looked like a painting in a museum.

"Jake and his family invited me out on their boat this afternoon."

"A sailboat?" his mother asked.

"I think it's more like a yacht."

"A yacht!" she hooted.

Toby couldn't tell if she was amused or skeptical but then, to his surprise, she turned to him and smiled in her distracted way. "Sure," she said. "Sounds like fun. Do you need to bring anything?"

"Jake said there'd be lunch on the boat."

"Fancy!" his mother teased and went back to her work.

Jake's parents and a friend were drinking cocktails as the *Snow-bird* slid past the breakwater to head out of the harbor. Toby's mother liked a glass of wine when they ate out. Toby's father didn't drink at all, though Toby had seen photos of him, glass in hand, back when he was younger and did. At restaurants he'd tell the waiter, "Just water," in a pointed way that Toby figured meant something, but he didn't know what.

Jake's mom and her friend reclined in twin swivel chairs at the stern. They wore bright lipstick, which Toby's mom never did, capris with crisp linen shirts. Their bracelets twinkled in the sun. Toby and Jake sat behind them on the swim platform, legs dangling, their fishing lines trailing in the boat's slow wake.

"So, is this like a real yacht?" Toby asked.

"Is this a yacht?" Jake laughed. He saw that his friend was serious. "No, man. It's a thirty-foot cabin cruiser. You have to be like super rich to own a yacht. You thought this was a yacht?"

Toby shrugged. "I guess not. I haven't been on that many boats."

"But you live on the ocean."

Toby saw that seemed baffling to Jake. He tried to make a joke. "Crazy, right?"

He heard Jake's mother tell her friend, "Toby's a local. From the house next door."

"That house?" The friend laughed, and Jake's mother did, too.

"We rented for the summer online," Jake's mom said quietly. "What can you tell from photos?"

In the warm sunlight, the purr of the boat created a lulling sound.

"What did she mean when she said 'that house'?" Toby repeated as a question to Jake.

Jake looked at him as though Toby should know the answer.

"I don't get it," Toby said.

Jake threw one arm around Toby's shoulders. "Your house is kind of a wreck. Right, man?"

Toby didn't know that his house was a wreck. The house was his house, but in Jake's words, he saw it from this city family's eyes. The peeling paint, the sagging front railing that his father never got around to fixing.

"Our house is worth a half million dollars!" he blurted out, rising to his family's defense. Toby had heard his parents say that once, when they were talking in the kitchen, and the sum sounded like a fortune to him. He thought that must mean they were millionaires.

Jake shook his head as though waiting for Toby to acknowledge the joke but that didn't happen.

"Really, dude?" He slapped him on the back. "I guess they're not spending any of that on home maintenance!"

Jake's mother and her friend exchanged glances. Jake's father, who was perched on his captain's chair behind the wheel, turned around to silence his son with a frown. Jake's mother refilled their glasses, accompanied by a jangle of ice cubes. The father returned to scanning the bay while his son concentrated on his fishing line with new seriousness. Toby understood then. Jake's family thought his parents were poor or slobs or negligent, or all three.

"I'm going for a swim!" he decided, stripping off his T-shirt and balling it on the deck. He was aware of his ribs protruding from his chest, but he didn't care. He kicked off his sandals.

"Where are you going to swim?" Jake looked bewildered as though they were not on a boat, surrounded by water.

"In the ocean."

Toby dove in, the shock of the cold Atlantic jolting him into motion. "Home," he shouted and plunged his face into the waves as voices from the big boat followed. Jake's mother stood at the side rail, glass in one hand. She cupped the other and called down, "You can't swim home. It's over a mile to shore."

Toby flipped on his back, arms thrusting behind him, powering him away. Jake and his mother leaned over the rail as the bobbing boat receded.

"It's too far," Jake's mother called. "You'll drown."

"No, I won't." Toby lifted his head from the water. "It's my ocean!" The faces on the boat diminished as their voices grew more demanding. "I live here!" Toby switched to his sidestroke, which he knew would carry him home. He concentrated on the shore, small figures on a blanket on the beach, the strength of his arms against the water, making him whole.

The boat tailed after him, Jake calling now, too. "Come on, man. Don't be like that." Jake's father turned back only when the water grew too shallow. Toby decided they must have realized he'd make it the rest of the way.

Toby emerged from the waves, exhausted, freezing. The distant figures he'd seen on the shore turned out to be a girl Toby used to know from school with her mother and younger sister, sitting on the little crescent beach. He realized they would have been watching him for a long time as he made his slow swim from the boat. The girl, whom he hadn't seen since fifth grade, wore a bright blue bikini. Toby didn't remember her name. She lifted her head briefly and then lay back on the blanket, a weary arm over her eyes.

Her mother seemed more concerned. She offered Toby the little girl's princess towel. Toby shook his head. She handed him a water bottle. "What were you doing out that far?" the mother asked.

Toby shrugged. "It didn't seem that far."

"Were you swimming from that boat?"

"Yeah." He turned toward the coast road. "Thanks for the water."

"Let us drive you home," the mother said.

"No, I'm good. I'll walk," Toby said.

"All right, here. How about a T-shirt, at least?"

She handed him one of hers and he put it on.

"Thanks."

"You're sure about the ride?" she called after him.

"I need to walk."

Toby didn't want to admit that what Jake and his mother said was true. His house did look a little ragged as he rounded the street to see it from afar. An upstairs shutter was still missing slats after a hurricane the year before; the lawn needed mowing. That was Toby's fault. He was supposed to have cut the grass on Saturday.

His mother was at the kitchen table hunched over one of her notebooks when Toby came through the back door, hours earlier than he'd told her he'd be home. She looked up with the unfocused glance she had when she was working on a poem. "What happened?"

"Nothing."

"I thought Jake's family was bringing you back after lunch. How did you get home?"

"I walked," Toby said.

"You walked! From where?"

"Quail Beach."

"The beach! You don't have any shoes."

"It was mostly grass."

His mother turned full around to face him. "What happened to your sandals?"

"I lost them." He hoped she wouldn't ask how. "I'm sorry."

Toby's mother put down her pencil and fixed him with a penetrating look she could summon when needed. "I thought you were on a boat, with the people next door."

"I swam back to shore."

"You swam? Toby, what happened?"

"Nothing."

"Something must have happened."

"Mom," Toby said.

She sighed. "Okay. Keep your secrets. You'll tell me if something is ever really wrong?"

"Of course I will."

Toby loved this about his mother. She always knew when to stop pressing. But as he stood by the refrigerator, Toby saw that the kitchen needed painting, too, as did the window frames above the sink which no longer opened no matter how hard his father shoved in sweltering summers. Shabbiness he'd never noticed before hung over everything, seen now from the rich people's eyes, but when Toby opened the fridge, his favorite brand of yogurt was there, the expensive kind; his mother must have been to the store. What did Jake and his stupid family know? They weren't poor.

Toby grabbed a bottle of juice. "Boats are boring."

"Of course they are," his mother said.

"What's for dinner?"

"I don't know." She gazed out the window. "I haven't thought about it."

"Dinner's boring."

"It is." She reached up to tousle his hair as he stood above her. "We'll scrounge up something in a while."

"I know we will."

His mother sighed. "You know, I am counting the days until summer is over and that cottage is empty again and we have our peace back."

"You say that every year."

"I shouldn't, though. Not this year. You're going to miss Jake when he leaves. I know you two were friends."

Toby paused in the doorway, the weight of the day releasing him into the solace of his mother's kitchen, her pottery on the windowsill, bright crimson walls painted before he was born.

He turned to head upstairs. "We were never friends."

CHAPTER 10

Party in the Woods

THE LITTLE RENTAL COTTAGE was so crummy it didn't have air conditioning. "There's a sea breeze," her father said. "You don't need air conditioning."

"*You* don't need air conditioning," Bree shot back. "It's a sauna in here."

She'd known from the outset this vacation would suck. The first night she hung a poster on the cottage wall and her father freaked out. So she used pushpins. "Do you not understand?" He loomed in the doorway. "This isn't your bedroom at home. We're renting. We put down a security deposit."

Bree looked up from her phone. "What, like a hundred dollars?"

"Fifteen hundred dollars!"

Bree tallied what that could buy. Things she needed, for example. Her parents had fifteen hundred dollars for a *security deposit* for a one-week vacation in the middle of nowhere. Why did her parents want to waste a week of their lives here year after year? Every afternoon, just for something to do, she hiked a mile and a half into the little tourist center you couldn't even call a town. Tacky fudge shops and T-shirt stores; other snooze places selling souvenirs and antiques. How did kids stand it here? Nowhere to go, nothing to buy besides candy and tourist junk.

Bree trudged along the sidewalk, counting the hours until the vacation was over and they'd be back in Connecticut where she had friends and a life. Loud rap music thumped through open windows coming from a car behind her. Bree tossed her crimson hair and checked out the driver over her shoulder, flashing the half smile she'd practiced in her mirror, but the car sped by. They didn't even honk. Losers.

In town, she bought a bag of overpriced fudge at the Chocolate Factory and inhaled the whole quarter pound on a bench by the harbor. Afterwards, she made herself throw up in the stinky public bathroom. A warning sign, "Shower At Your Own Risk," hung on the wall. Where was she, the Bates Motel? A woman outside Bree's stall tapped softly on the latched door, all concerned. "Are you all right, honey?"

"No, I'm dying," Bree snorted and then burst out laughing. She heard the woman shuffle away, and she felt a little bad about that. She waited until the heavy metal outside door clanged shut, then waited another five minutes before she thought it safe to venture back outside. She rinsed her mouth at the sink and unwrapped a stick of chewing gum. An old woman in a shapeless dress and floppy red sun hat leaned against the railing, waiting for her. Bree recognized her chunky sandals.

"It's all a joke to you now, isn't it?" she said. "Life's a joke." The woman had a kind voice, but her expression wasn't. "You'll die, too, one day, you know. You might not believe it, but you *will*."

That really bummed her. Bree slid on her sunglasses and fixed her barely chewed gum beneath the railing. That felt good for a minute but once she turned the corner, she felt the tears descend. Sometimes she didn't know why she did the things she did.

Back at the cottage, she was bored again, bored with the town, bored with hanging around her claustrophobic room off the kitchen. Her creepy little cousins had arrived and she was supposed to entertain them. That was ridiculous. She was fifteen and the nerdy little twins were eight. To amuse herself, Bree flirted with the dad next door instead. He sat outside in a lawn chair under a tree, reading a book. He still read library books! She could tell by the shiny cellophane cover. It was like being dropped into the previous century.

Bree took her time bending over in her short shorts, doing stretches on the lawn in his line of vision. She turned her back on him then, lazily spreading her legs wide and bending low from the waist, pretending to do yoga, her little white shorts riding up, exposing her firm butt cheeks.

It's not like in a million years she would want him to touch her. Or his teenage son. She'd seen him up there, lurking at one of the upstairs windows. She didn't really want to flirt with either one. She was restless and it was a game. Besides, he never looked up. Afterwards, she ate half a bag of Oreos, then made herself throw up in the cottage's single bathroom, hoping her mother didn't hear. She knew she was pathetic.

She told them she had a headache but of course they didn't care. Her parents forced her to go with them on a whale watch the next day. As they steamed out of the marina, Bree had to admit the town looked cute from afar. Pastel-colored houses climbed the streets overlooking the harbor. New England church steeples dotted the hill.

Bree flirted with the young deckhands giving her the eye, trying to ignore the stupid lecture over the PA. What did she care what the whales ate, what their nicknames were. They were endangered. They got entangled in fishing gear. That was sad. But was this high school? If she wanted to learn about whales, she'd Google it.

She hoped the hot staff guys knew she wasn't like the rest of the out-of-town tourists they saw every day, frantically rushing from port to starboard like a flock of dumb birds spooked by the wind. But then Bree saw her first whale rise out of the water—a gigantic grinning sea monster—a spray of Atlantic mist and whale breath showering her face. A whale!

Close-up it was like something escaped from another universe, playfully arcing its massive back beneath the sunlight before it waved its tail, as though to Bree alone, and disappeared beneath the sea once more. She felt something then. She hadn't in a long time.

Her shrink at home liked to talk about body issues and shame, but Bree didn't think that was it. She didn't feel ashamed. She didn't even make herself hurl that often anymore; she could stop if she wanted to. Bree had always known that was true. She just didn't want to.

Anyway, she wasn't the only one of her Connecticut friends who did it. They all did, a secret rite of passage. She pictured

them now, Julie and Susanna and Riley, the pack of them carous-
ing through gloomy suburban streets. Loud, boisterous, intentionally obnoxious. Bree in the purple wig her parents didn't
know she had, seeing as she wasn't allowed to dye her hair until
she was eighteen, though people told her why should she dye it,
when her hair was already awesome? Because she could!

To score at their game, they had to make a passing adult
shake their heads or take a second glance, flashing disapprov-
ing looks. The best was when their target actually engaged.
Then Bree—whose real name was Breyleigh, though her fabu-
lous friends had shortened it to Bree for brilliant—Bree would
shout back a stream of nonsensical words or a line of poetry,
just to see the bewilderment on their faces. You could tell they
were expecting a profanity, some mindless teenage sass—but
Bree's friends said her genius was never to give them what they
were expecting. She messed with their minds. Which was ironic,
considering her own was basically a wreck.

On the final day of vacation, the adults took the cousins to
play miniature golf a few towns away, and Bree had the day to
herself. She strolled into town, thinking she'd gorge on another
bag of taffy or fudge and maybe puke it up, or maybe not, but
once she got there, she sat on the breakwater, cross-legged on
the warm New England granite, debating with herself if that
was a bad idea.

A boy in an open flannel shirt sauntered by, then stopped to
squat beside her. He nodded in greeting. "I've seen you around."

"Yeah, I'm here all right."

"But you're not from here."

"God, no."

"Right. It's a drag."

Bree swiveled her glance. He was skinny with longish hair, but kind of cute in a sad-sack sort of way. She liked his smile. "So what do you do for fun?"

"Not much." He shrugged. "Not usually. There's a party in the woods at the quarry tonight, though. You want to come?"

"What kind of party?"

"You know."

Bree shook her head. "I don't."

"Someone older who doesn't give a shit buys beer. We build a fire. Play music. Get wasted. Whatever."

Bree thought it sounded lame, but what else was she doing? "Yeah, I guess."

His name was Fred. They arranged to meet at the convenience store at eight. Bree told her parents she'd be watching *Star Trek* at the library. Sometimes she was amazed at the shit they'd believe.

Fred drove an old Jeep that must have been his mom's. An air freshener in the shape of a rose swung from the rearview mirror. They quickly exhausted all conversation—where she lived in Connecticut, what kind of music she listened to. Fred turned up the radio and they rode in silence. Bree snuck quick glances from the passenger seat and decided she wouldn't kiss him.

He parked on a dirt road, and they hiked the rest of the way through some woods to a small clearing near the quarry. Loud rock from a band she didn't recognize blared from a boom box. A dozen or so shadowy faces huddled around a small camp-fire. Kids here still had boom boxes! Fred grabbed two beers from a cooler, and they sat together on a tree stump. He didn't introduce her to anyone, not that she cared. She wished she hadn't come.

After another beer and a plastic cup of grape juice and vodka that Fred called "Purple Passion," Bree changed her mind. She and Fred had nothing to say but the music got better. The laughter around the circle sounded grown-up and free. Couples angled closer in the dark. Someone was making s'mores over the flames, which seemed like the best thing she'd ever tasted. When Fred moved in for a kiss, she didn't push him away as she'd planned. His mouth tasted like marshmallows and Hershey's chocolate which was nice, but then his hand was snaking under her shirt which she didn't like.

The revving engine of a pickup charging up the road stole his attention, and Bree used the opportunity to scoot apart. Fred turned toward the sound. Around the circle, other faces glanced up as well.

"Shit." Fred stared at his feet.

"What?"

"These jerks."

Three older boys emerged from the woods into the clearing. They stood with arms crossed surveying the scene. The ringleader's gaze rested briefly on Bree. She leaned into Fred. "Maybe we should go," she said.

"Nah." He shrugged. "I want to see what happens."

"Hey fat face." The lead boy found who he was searching for, a pudgy kid in plaid shorts that looked a couple sizes too big for him. His accoster hauled the kid to his feet. "I've got something for you." He punched the boy in the face, then wiped his hands on his ripped T-shirt as though he'd dirtied them.

The kid reeled back a few steps but didn't fall. A new quiet descended on the party. "Be glad you didn't really piss me off," the tough boy said.

"What did I do?"

"Ask Mr. Evans."

Bree whispered, "Who's Mr. Evans?"

"The principal," Fred said.

"This is stupid," Bree decided. "Your friends are stupid."

"They're not my friends."

Bree jabbed him in the arm. "I'm ready to go home."

"So go."

"Aren't you going to drive me?"

"It's not that far."

Bree couldn't believe it. "You're really a loser."

"You're a spoiled brat."

She stood to leave, and the lead boy nodded at her across the fire. "Hey little hottie, what are you doing over there with Dead Fred?"

"Nothing," Bree said. "I'm leaving."

The leader's sidekick took a long swig of vodka. "Okay, bro. Party time!" He lurched around the circle, peering at the gathered faces. "Who wants to party?"

A dark-haired Latina girl giggled, and he swooped her into in his arms—the girl laughing or crying, Bree couldn't tell—as he staggered with her back into the woods. Around the circle, the other girls averted their gaze. Bree took her seat again next to Fred. "I'm scared. I mean it. We should go."

He looked at her as though he hadn't seen her before. "Go where? Go home? It's not even eleven o'clock."

The boy who'd punched the fat kid picked out a slinky red-haired girl in cut-off shorts and a halter top. He reached down to pull her toward him by her hands and they swayed together by the fire. The girl was smiling but she didn't look happy. Bree thought about calling her father, but they were having a party on their last night at the cottage, her father and his brother and one of their business friends from Hartford.

A scream rose from the woods. Maybe not a scream. A girl's voice, excited and shrill. The boy in the ripped T-shirt turned his back on the party, unzipped his jeans, and began peeing into the woods.

"I need to do that, too," Bree said. "I need to pee."

Fred made a face. "Gross. What do I care?"

"What's wrong with you?" Bree got to her feet, legs shaking, on the verge of tears. "You're a total fuck."

Fred laughed. "As if."

The boy peeing at the edge of the woods zipped his pants and lunged for Bree as she stumbled past. Now that she was moving, she realized how unsteady she was, but the boy was drunker and lost his balance as she pulled free.

Bree took off at a run, the boy's voice behind her, increasingly angry. "Hey, where you going? Come back here. Hey! I'm talking to you. Bitch!"

Bree crashed into the woods, clutching at trees to keep her balance. She remembered Fred had left his keys in the ignition when they parked his mother's Jeep. At the time, she'd thought this was further proof how lame this town must be. People not only didn't lock cars, they left their keys inside, because no one would steal your car here, the place was that out of it—but now she was shaking with joy as she slid behind the wheel, or rather fell sideways into the driver's seat, completely bombed. She managed to right herself, slamming the car into reverse and peeling away.

Shouts echoed through the woods after her, but she was behind the wheel now and she had to get away. She'd seldom driven a car, a few times in a parking lot with her dad. Blindly, she careened down the rutted dirt road, terrified someone would catch up to her, one of the enormous pickups parked up at the clearing, barreling behind her, forcing her off the road.

Bree pressed the pedal to the floor at the same moment she saw the wavering shadow in the middle of the dirt path and felt the unmistakable bump as she drove over it. An animal? God, she hoped not. She loved animals. There was no sound, so maybe she imagined she'd hit something. A rock or a tree stump like the one Fred had swerved to avoid hours earlier. She felt better remembering that, the innocence of their earlier drive down this same road, how she'd bounced around in the passenger seat beside him like they were riding bumper cars.

She knew she should turn back to make sure she hadn't hit anything, but how could she, when those boys could be right behind her? Bree kept going, hurtling down the dirt path, slowing down only when she reached the paved road where she hugged the white line of the bicycle lane, trying not to hit the curb. There was no traffic, no one out. Bree made the turn into the cottage lane, though she didn't know how she remembered the right street in the dark.

She jerked the car into the driveway and rolled to a stop halfway up the lawn. She was drunk. And her parents would be pissed. There'd be "consequences" this time, for sure, as her father liked to warn. Back home in Connecticut, when she and her friends pulled some outrageous prank, they'd shriek and run away, daring someone to come after them, but no one ever cared enough to catch them. Not once. They'd always gotten away.

Outside the car, she steadied herself against the door. Bree willed herself not to see anything, but she did. The grill was badly dented; under the moonlight, something fluttered in the breeze. A piece of bright fabric. She'd hit someone. It wasn't a rock or a tree stump or even a deer, which would have been horrible but okay. She pulled out the flashlight on her phone and saw the cloth stuck to the grill was splattered in blood.

The figure in the road. The laughing-crying older girl carried into the woods. The cloth was part of her T-shirt. The girl had gotten free. She was running away.

Bree knew then what she'd done. She sunk to her knees and vomited on the lawn, not like she did with her finger down her throat in the town bathroom, or the times before kneeling over her toilet at home, but violently, totally, her insides heaving, the grape juice and vodka, the reeking beers, the hamburger she'd eaten that day and finally, the multiple s'mores she'd downed fresh off the fire, before anything terrible happened. The contents of her stomach pooled at her feet, a colorful, putrid mess, bile burned down her throat. What had she done? Killed someone?

She vomited again, the last of all she'd consumed, and wiped her mouth on her sleeve, leaving a raw purple slash across her favorite lacy top, as if that was important anymore. When she lurched through the front door, her father was already storming down the hall from the kitchen. He came to a stop, his hands firmly on his hips. "Where the hell were you?" He leveled her with a stern gaze. "Breyleigh—"

Her father never called her that anymore. She sunk to her knees. "Something happened, Daddy. Something awful."

"Did someone hurt you?"

"No, no." The faces in the firelight came back to her, the girl being dragged away, how easily it could have been her.

"Why are you crying?" His face looked like he did when he was about to start yelling, but Bree's tears made him waver.

He didn't know yet, and that made her feel even worse, if that was possible.

He still lived in the world that just ended.

CHAPTER 11

Alone

HE HADN'T BEEN ASLEEP LONG when flashing blue lights pulled him from a dream. For a fleeting moment, Tom thought those emergency lights might be for him. But why would they be?

It was the police, three patrol cars at the cottage next door. The cop in the driveway shot a stern gaze above the hedge when he noticed Tom gazing down from his upstairs window. Seeing himself discovered, he turned out the light and retreated to his study down the hall to be less visible. As though he were guilty, as though he were the one who'd done something wrong. Instinctively, fear was his response to any crisis.

He should get away from the window, stop watching whatever calamity was unfolding below, but he found it impossible to turn away. Those lights catapulted him back to the fire, blue lights flashing on the grass, and he was twenty-four again, wandering through Harvard Yard, Cat's bewildered face lit by emergency lights.

His shift that night had been nearly over. He'd been mindlessly shelving books in the Widener stacks when he came face to face with his father's name. He found himself standing before the section that housed Noah Osborne's works. The loathsome title he remembered as a teenager was one of them. As a punishment for some infraction—he couldn't recall what—his father had forced him to compile an index of his manuscript in progress: *Contemplative Paradox: Seven Treatises and a Digression on Dante.*

The tedium of reading through those typewritten pages, taking notes, making lists, was an experience he never forgot. But Tom had been pleased to note, he'd done a better job at sixteen than the indexer the academic publisher ultimately hired. He compared both versions when the treatise came out that fall, deriving grim satisfaction though not his father's acknowledgment.

The absurdity and injustice of it all, of the disdain he still felt from his father, rushed back to him that night in the stacks. Before he knew what he was doing, or even why, Tom was taking down those mighty tomes from the shelves, piling them on the floor, and with them, his life as he once envisioned it. Scholar, thinker, success. His name embossed on the spines of other well-received books. His life would never turn out that way, and he already knew that was true.

Coulda been the right place, musta been the wrong time. When had it ever not been the wrong time? If only. If never. Not to be. Noah Osborne had shackled his son to his misery in ways Tom would never understand. How had he done this? Tom didn't know, but he felt it was true. Screw his father. And the library. Screw Harvard and the wasted years of his life. What could he do?

He reached into his pocket and there it was, a matchbook.

Tom had recently started bumming cigarettes from strangers. He'd approach, matchbook ready, offering a light to smokers stepping out of the wind or struggling with book bags or groceries, scrambling to find a lighter, cigarette in hand.

"May I?" He saw himself as a character in a movie, which allowed him to deploy his next line. "Would you mind if I bummed one?" Sometimes he added that he was trying to quit, which wasn't true. He was trying not to get started.

Tom thumbed through *Contemplative Paradox*, fanning all six hundred and fifty pages which smelled vaguely of someone's basement. He ran his finger down the index. He lit a match.

The spark for all that followed.

He liked to think he'd done his best to be a good father to Toby. He hoped he had, though God knows he'd always feared his inadequacy as a parent, having grown up haunted by his own. Sometimes, when he was feeling generous, Tom remembered that his father battled darkness, too.

He'd discovered this as a revelation one afternoon when he was ten and returned home to find his father crouched in the angled space beneath the staircase, a favorite place Tom liked to play when he was small. As a child, he'd loved the intricate carved woodwork beneath the banister, the sense of hiding in a secret compartment beneath the world.

Tom's father was hunched over with his back to the front door, his knees clasped to his chest, face buried in his arms. If he heard his son come in, he gave no indication. Tom's mother was in the kitchen.

"Good," she said when Tom told her where he was. "He can stay there."

"But what's he doing? Is Dad hiding?"

"Why don't you ask him?"

"He shouldn't be there," Tom persisted, and his mother softened slightly at the mounting concern in his voice.

"Maybe that's where your father does his thinking, Tom-Tom. He must like it there. It's his cave."

If his father's illness had a name, it was never acknowledged. Tom wondered if anyone aside from his mother was even aware. In his professional life, he'd managed to rise above all that pulled Tom down. Youngest Classics PhD in Harvard's history, lured away by the English chairman as a prize. Tenure by thirty-five. Tom's illness broke him before he ever began.

Flashing police lights continued to strobe along the upstairs hall. How could Toby manage to sleep through it all? He could sleep through anything. Tom envied his capacity for oblivion.

Catharine was at a poetry workshop in Ireland, but Tom well imagined her howl of protest. What had this latest crop of unspeakable, annoying renters unleashed on their falling-down paradise. *What now?* his wife would cry if she were here.

The view from his second-floor study was a distant ribbon of the Atlantic. All that could be seen of the coast this late at night was the faint green glow of a lighthouse forlornly blinking through the trees. Witnessing the scene below, Tom wished as he often had over the years: if only they'd been able to buy that little cottage any of the times it had gone on the market over the years.

They'd watch the "For Sale" sign periodically appear at the curb and quake in dread each time the place changed hands. If only they'd been the landlords, they might have tamed the weekly turmoil of vacationers.

The lighthouse beam swung back into view, the pulsing beacon his father's ridicule made him hate.

"If it isn't Gatsby's green light!" Noah Osborne sardonically named it the first time he and Tom's mother visited.

"Oh Noah!" His mother laughed. Encouraging him. As she always did.

At their wedding, Tom watched with dread as she pulled aside his new wife to whisper something in her ear. Catharine would never confess what she'd said, not all these years later—*I don't remember*, she'd protest whenever he brought it up—but he knew she must.

He'd seen the impact of those words from across the room, his new wife's expression, her physical recoil from whatever her mother-in-law had told her. What terrible thing might Polly Osborne have laid upon the woman who married her son?

Sometimes, he wondered if whatever she'd whispered could have been the seed that ruined their future, a fairytale curse imparted from the lips of his mother in their first hours as man and wife.

And yet faithful Catharine still strove each day to keep their bobbing ship afloat. Soon, he knew, he'd let her down again. He could feel it starting again, the darkness closing in. He'd done so well. He'd done so well for so long, he almost let himself imagine it was over. No more episodes. Tom stood at the window, wondering how long he could stave off what he knew would follow. Each descent worse than the last.

Catharine was flying home tomorrow after ten days away, maybe in the air even now. What time was it in Dublin? Five hours ahead. Four-thirty in the morning. She'd still be asleep in the little hotel across from the National Library, the bargain she'd been thrilled to discover from someone's blog.

Morbid thoughts visited him sometimes when she was gone, when he was alone. When he woke to the police lights earlier, one of his first thoughts was: could they have come because of Catharine, the police here to tell him her plane had crashed? For a moment, he allowed himself to imagine that future.

Their marriage had been impossible, maybe more times than not. Their marriage impossible, and yet they'd survived. *Tomcat went the distance!* How many decades? How many left. More and more his thoughts seemed to wander to the borderline, the edge of the beyond. What was out there?

Is that all there is? the old song used to moan. *Then keep dancing*—is that how it went?

Tom did a quick backwards waltz away from the window in his study. And then? He couldn't remember the rest. His overwhelming sense of fatigue took over, a sensation of being held underwater.

He wished he could will himself out of bed before eleven those mornings he didn't have to teach that summer, or that he felt like getting dressed, shaving, showering. Living? Was he tired of living? Some days he was.

"How about a bath?" Catharine would ask from the doorway when he hadn't gotten dressed in days. Surely he could manage a bath. Hot water, steam. His bones at rest. It might feel good. Her concerned face hovered in the threshold day after day, offering inducements. How about a grilled cheese?

Tomato soup? A cup of tea with buttered toast? I bought your favorite ice cream. Noble all-giving Catharine. So many years. Their whole marriage if he were honest. He could do that for her. He could take a bath. Instead, too often, he'd close his eyes to drift back to sleep a little longer.

Maybe they shouldn't have tried so hard to stay together. He didn't blame Catharine. Neither of them was to blame. Marriage was hard. Life was hard, had always been hard. Tom heard his father mocking him for those words. The brilliant Dr. Osborne. His mother like a hummingbird by his side. Patrice who rechristened herself Polly. Always chipper. The antidote to Dr. NO, who was never chipper. Life is hard? Tom heard his father's voice in his head, berating him as though he were in the room. Listen to yourself. Could you entertain a shallower thought, son?

Tom had done a better job at parenthood than his own father. He had. He could be thankful for that. And yet, how rare were the times he and Toby spent together anymore. He didn't know if either he or Catharine really knew their son. Toby held a part of himself locked away, accessible to no one. Tom didn't blame him.

Over the years, his boy had overheard things he shouldn't have, things he and Catharine had said to one another. You couldn't call them arguments, exactly. They were proud that they never screamed at each other, as some couples do, and yet: the pointed barbs they'd hurl. Tom was sure their son had heard more than he should have.

He'd tried to shield Toby, to protect him where he could, to hold himself together for his son. That time at the Christmas

Revels long ago, little Toby on his shoulders, the two of them careening through the lobby of Sanders Theatre. The place where Tom had leapt from the balcony years before. That day with Toby balanced on his shoulders, he'd sensed the terrifying abyss begin to open below, and felt himself losing focus, almost letting his grip on his son go. Somehow, he'd willed himself back to consciousness, salvaging the moment, knowing Cat would kill him, literally she would, if anything ever happened to Toby that was his fault. His wife would never forgive him, and he wouldn't forgive himself. Toby was their world, the life they'd managed to create.

"Dad!" he heard his son call from down the hall. Tom hadn't been aware of him stirring in his room. There was a hint of fear in his son's voice. He must have gone into his parents' bedroom to find the bed empty, the covers pulled back.

"In here," Tom called.

Toby jogged down the hall and came to stand beside him at the window where the lights below still flashed. At fifteen, he was a head taller than Tom, his brown hair disheveled from sleep. Shirtless in boxer shorts, he looked muscular, more filled-out than Tom remembered. He smelled of sleep, summer sweat, the restaurant where he'd just started working.

"What's happening down there?" his son asked.

"I don't know."

"Three cop cars. Isn't that like the whole town?"

"I think there might be five."

Toby laughed. "No way. The town has five cop cars?"

"Keeping Belle Harbor safe."

As they stood by the window, suddenly the cottage door opened and a young girl was being led out of the house, followed by her father. Her arms were handcuffed behind her back.

"Wow," Toby said. "What did she do?"

Tom sighed. "Thank God your mom's not here."

"I know," Toby agreed. "Won't she love to hear about this, though?"

"You know she will."

"Another horror at the cottage!"

"The hated cottage."

Toby joked, "Maybe when no one's there this winter we should burn it down."

Tom turned on his son with alarm. "Don't ever say that!"

It was as though Toby had read his thoughts earlier reliving the night of the fire.

"Dad, I didn't mean it. Chill."

"It's not as if the guy in Florida wouldn't rebuild anyway," Tom said. "With insurance money."

Toby looked confused. "I'm not serious, Dad. Come on. I'm not going to burn down anything."

"Of course not." Tom tried to lighten the mood. "We'd just end up with an even bigger, more extravagant destination for obnoxious guests."

"Mom would love that."

They stood in silence for a few minutes, watching the first of the patrol cars back out of the driveway and flash its way down the quiet street. The lights were all ablaze in the little cottage, but no one was visible inside. Tom had seen the family earlier in the week. That afternoon, he was vaguely aware of the girl doing calisthenics on the lawn.

How quickly life can implode. As he had so many times before, Tom assured himself that there would have been signs by now, had Toby inherited his father's disease, the disease of Tom's father's before him. Though his wife would never admit it, Tom knew that Catharine feared this, too, that they both secretly prayed the curse would end with him. The last of the crazy Osbornes. Tom looked over at his son.

"I wonder what happened," Toby said.

"A small town harbors no secrets," Tom replied. "Ten bucks says we'll find out tomorrow." He fist-bumped his son's arm, aware of the muscles that hadn't been there the year before. "Don't you have to work in the morning? You should get some sleep."

"So should you."

"I'll try," Tom said. His son lingered for a moment in the doorway. "Goodnight, Tobe. Love you."

"Mean it." Toby smiled.

The rejoinder was an old joke between them. Tom had no idea where it came from. Maybe one of the music videos his son used to watch, a private world of arcane references.

The last of the no longer flashing police cruisers backed out of the drive next door and Tom watched the darkness descend, the stars blinking back overhead, the sound of the advancing high tide breaking in the nearby cove, the lighthouse with its arcing light.

Tomorrow Catharine would return. She'd be waking soon in Dublin, getting a cab to the airport. He hoped she'd found whatever she was looking for from the workshop, the creative epiphany she'd been anticipating all these months.

He envied her for this, too. Her dedication, discipline, the belief in her own promise that allowed her to apply for the program. He'd lost such hopes for himself long ago. Was Cat destined for disappointment, too, in whatever dreams she still carried? Who was he to say.

His medication smoothed everything out, all jagged edges gone, leaving mental gruel. Tom Osborne the promising young poet had become the man who felt nothing. Not even a glimmer of—oh!—for the young girl preening in her short shorts that afternoon, idly flirting with him from the lawn next door. Glancing up from his book, he'd been aware of her watching him, performing for him, and he'd felt not a flicker of interest. Temptation was one of the human emotions now safely beyond grasp, courtesy of his meds.

What had that girl gotten herself involved in hours later, to wind up arrested. Three police cars. Not that the cops in town had anything else to do. Tom was doubly glad now that he'd glanced up once and gone back to his book before she'd noticed his gaze, no acknowledgment between them, no involvement with the lives next door.

Tomorrow, he'd tell Catharine when she returned. An interesting story to share. Something had happened in sleepy Belle Harbor while she was gone.

He hoped his wife would be happy when she returned. She'd been looking forward to the conference for over a year. Or not unhappy, at least. Was that too much to hope for?

A new beginning.

Maybe they could start over, as they'd vowed so many times over the years.

Maybe they couldn't.

CHAPTER 12

Trinity

THEY MET AT THE YEATS EXHIBIT at the National Library near her hotel. He took a seat beside her in the little booth where a flat screen, framed by Celtic runes, played a continuous film loop called "The Other World." Spangled purple curtains framed the walls. Catharine felt as though she'd stepped into a seer's inner room, accompanying the poet and his friends on their esoteric journey.

A scent of pipe tobacco preceded him; she felt the damp rising from his wool coat. The man leaned toward her. "Do you suppose they truly made contact?" His tone sounded almost mocking, but when she glanced at his face, she saw he was serious. His accent wasn't Irish.

"With the beyond?" She smiled. "I imagine they thought so."

He was older than she was, in his fifties. His face thoughtfully lined behind dark-framed glasses; a long, straight nose, a handsome profile in the dim light. "You're American?" The man sounded surprised.

"And you're not Irish."

"Scots." A flickering video image reflected off his glasses. On the screen, a woman with piercing eyes gazed from beneath a turban; veiled dancers flitted behind her. "Are you familiar with *A Vision?*"

"W.B.'s book of automatic writing?" Catharine had tried to read Yeats's spiritual memoir several times. "I've never gotten through it, actually."

He laughed. "Nor I."

"I've meant to. He was a brilliant poet. My favorite perhaps," Catharine hurried to add as though she'd dishonored Yeats's memory, here in this room, sacred with his things.

"An intriguing man," the stranger agreed. "Pursuing Maud Gonne all those decades. Holding fast to heartbreak."

Catharine loved the phrase. It made her think of her husband. *Holding fast to heartbreak.* What would Tom be doing this hour in Massachusetts? Eight a.m. He taught part-time in the summer, so he'd either be on his way to work in the city, or trying to get himself out of bed. Toby, she imagined, would be deep in dreams, still asleep.

"I admire their commitment," Catharine said. "Their belief. Don't you?"

"Of course."

"There's a photo beneath the case over there of Maud Gonne. Did you see it?"

Catharine had. A beautiful dark-haired woman, haughty eyed beneath the glass case. Yeats's lifelong unanswered love. Her hand-on-hip portrait was placed between an Abbey Theatre flyer and a sun-drenched chalice. Maud Gonne, revolutionary, mystic, legendary beauty—the poet's muse.

Catharine glanced around the darkened room, the sparkling curtains catching the light, the soft murmur of videos with their voices of the past. "This room could be the scene of a séance."

"You speak from experience?"

She turned from the screen and laughed. "No. Never."

"Perhaps we might find one then?"

"I don't know Dublin," she said.

"Ah, but I do."

"You're from Dublin?"

He extended his hand. "Gavin Royce. I teach up the road here at Trinity."

"Catharine Osborne." His hand was strong and rough as though he worked outdoors and not in a lecture hall. "I'm at Trinity myself. Only for the week. A poetry workshop."

"You write poetry," the man said.

Catharine no longer knew if what she wrote could be called poetry. Her pages seemed more like a journal now, a confessional. The workshop, in fact, had been mostly a disaster. The half-dozen attendees were all young. She was aware they made plans with each other in the evenings that didn't include her. The teacher was another disappointment. The celebrated poet Archie Dent recited from his own work in a monotone, issued a perfunctory assignment, snapped his briefcase shut at the end of three hours and disappeared until the following afternoon. Not what she'd saved for all year.

"I do write poetry," Catharine answered. "And what do you teach?"

"Existential Philosophy."

"Really?"

"No." His laughter pealed through the quiet room. "Geology. Quite boring."

"I'm sure it's not."

"No, but Tuesdays generally are. Five-hour break between classes. Often, I wander over here to draw a bit of sustenance from our friend W.B., as you call him. Then I lift a glass or two at the Shelbourne and indulge in a bit of people watching."

"I do that, too. Well, people watching."

"Perhaps you'll join me?"

A glass of wine in a hotel bar with a stranger. There was nothing wrong in that, and yet Catharine wondered if there was. Lonely all week, she'd been starved for conversation, already wishing that she hadn't come to Dublin, that she'd spent the money on something else. Something they needed for the house, for example. A new dishwasher. An appliance to validate the ordinariness of her existence, the absurdity of thinking she was a real poet, or would ever be.

As she rose from the stone bench, her hand rested on a carved object. In the dim light, she barely made it out. When she bent closer, Catharine saw it was a gargoyle.

"That would be lovely," she said.

"Red or white?" Gavin Royce asked after they were settled at a window in the hotel bar.

Catharine said white and he ordered a bottle. *A bottle, not a glass?* The waiter delivered it in a silver bucket on a stand, a white cloth over his arm. Catharine looked across at St. Stephen's Green, yellow double-decker buses trundling past outside the tall windows overlooking the street. She thought again of Tom and their son, what they'd be doing. What was she doing?

"See that couple over there?" Gavin pointed to a booth where a woman in a black dress and a long string of pearls huddled with a much younger man, both of them engaged in lively conversation. The woman crossed her legs and brushed against her companion's each time she laughed.

"What about them?"

"He's with a different woman every Tuesday."

"So, you are here every Tuesday."

"It's my weekly reward." He raised his glass as though offering a toast.

"What do you suppose the regulars might be thinking about you then?"

She realized the question sounded more provocative than she'd intended. She felt herself blush.

Gavin refilled her glass. "I wouldn't dare to speculate. Actually," he said, "I'm very unexciting. I'm always here alone. Tell me about your poetry."

"It isn't much."

"You shouldn't say that."

Catharine agreed. "Yes, I know. I should have more confidence."

"Shall we try again?" He leaned forward. "Tell me about your poetry."

For the first time in years, the week in Dublin had provided uninterrupted days to consider her life as a poet. Writing poetry was one of the dozen things Catharine did each day and usually the one to receive the least time.

She'd had that one small success in the contest long ago. Every once in a while, a published poem in a journal when she could find the time to send one out. There was always Tom's illness, his needs, her son's, the demands of being a mother, her job as a teacher.

This week at the conference she'd found herself wondering: even without all that, would it have mattered? What was it she burned to say?

"My poetry," Catharine finally answered. "The summers, really, that's the only real time I have."

"And the rest of the year?"

"I teach. I have a family."

"Ah, the family."

"And you?"

"You already know I teach. But no. I have no family."

"None?"

"Oh, brothers and sisters, cousins, aunts and uncles. Scads. My parents are dead. But family of my own, the wife and babes—that life, sadly, eluded me."

Catharine couldn't tell if he was serious. "I have a son," she said. "Toby. He's fifteen. And a husband."

"A lucky man."

Catharine laughed.

"He's unlucky then?" he asked with a comic lilt.

"I don't know about luck," she said. "I doubt he'd consider himself lucky. A casualty of karma maybe."

"He has bad karma?"

The realization this man was invoking her husband to flirt with her settled with unease. She pictured Tom sipping a beer on their deck, locking up the house, turning out the porch light.

Though the time was wrong for all that. It wasn't even lunch-time at home.

Catharine often wondered if she'd known before she married Tom, before they had Toby, if she'd known how deep the vein of his illness ran, would she have bound her life to his? She wasn't sure. Catharine still believed Tom could have done all those things, the brilliant plans of his youth. If not for the fact he was bipolar. And for herself—what of her brilliant plans? Catharine reached for her wine and Gavin refilled the glass.

"So, it's bad karma then?" This time his question no longer sounded like a joke though the permanent amusement of his mouth made it seem like one.

"You're very clever," Catharine said.

"It's the wine."

He assessed her with a conspiratorial smile as though they were not strangers. Catharine met his gaze. "Do you often pick up women in libraries? On your Tuesdays."

"Is that what you think this is?"

"I don't know what it is."

"Neither do I."

A waiter dropped a small tray of glasses across the room. Other heads turned, but Gavin's didn't. His earnest attention wouldn't let her look away. "Why did you approach me at the exhibit?" she asked.

"You seemed interesting."

"I was watching a video on automatic writing."

"Well, yes." He rotated the bottle in its silver holder as though examining the label. "Do you believe some things in life are meant to be?"

"I believe in reincarnation," Catharine said. "I guess that's somewhat the same."

Gavin crossed his arms. "I'm listening. Go on."

"I believe we've had other lives." Catharine took another sip of wine. "Will have future lives. As people, though. Not animals."

"Never animals," he said with a wry smile. "Nor insects."

"Definitely not insects."

"Have we met before then?"

"Possibly."

His voice was mock serious. "How many lifetimes?"

Catharine shook her head. "I couldn't guess."

"To be investigated?" Gavin glanced at his watch. "I need to teach my next class at half past five. May we continue the conversation?"

"I leave on Friday."

"Tomorrow then?"

Catharine wavered, not sure what he was asking, where it might lead. "Lunch?"

"It would have to be dinner." He signaled the waiter for the check. "I have classes all day Wednesday."

Catharine agreed, trying to sort through what she was agreeing to. If it was fine to share an afternoon glass of wine with another man, what about dinner? Would that be wrong? No, it wasn't. But if she felt something, even the slightest flutter of interest in an attractive man who, for whatever reason, found her interesting. Was that betraying Tom? No.

Not yet.

That thought chilled her. Catharine couldn't imagine meeting another man for dinner at home. Belle Harbor with its year-

round population of five thousand gossips. That was a freedom
that didn't exist. Would never exist. But here it did. She was
free in a way she'd never been, which seemed at the moment a
terrifying possibility.

They arranged to meet at the Nassau Street gate to Trinity. In
the lit windows of side street flats, Catharine saw a man reading the newspaper, a woman bouncing a baby, a vase of flowers
beneath a chandelier. A young girl set the table. She thought of
her husband and son across the ocean.

Gavin was waiting beside a shop window as she rounded
the corner of Dawson Street. Scarf knotted at his neck, a belted
raincoat, his briefcase at his feet. His dress and demeanor and
manners seemed so unlike the pattern of casual indifference she
and Tom had fallen into. He turned and spotted her. "I'm glad
you came."

"This must be my treat tonight," Catharine announced once
they were seated in an upstairs spot he knew near Temple Bar.

He waved her off with a smile. "What might not be evident,
Mrs. Osborne, is that it's my treat not to dine alone."

Catharine glanced around the softly lit tables, couples leaning into each other. A room full of private worlds. She wondered if Gavin was often alone.

"Is there a reason—," she asked, "why you never chose to
have a family?" She surprised herself by speaking the question
aloud. He smiled.

"Many reasons," he said. "Not all of them my choosing.
I was married for a time when I was younger. Divorced. No

children. And I was with someone for quite a while. She died last year."

"I'm sorry," Catharine said. "I shouldn't have asked."

"I like talking about her," Gavin replied. "Sinéad was her name. She had children. Two of them. Grown now. But I see them from time to time. So, I'm not a totally bereft old man."

"You're not old."

"But it's easy to feel that way sometimes, isn't it? Though you're no way near those sentiments. You're a young woman still."

"I'm forty-five."

"I'm fifty-eight. It's only been since Sinéad died that it begins to occur to me—the future is no longer an open road, is it?"

Never once had Catharine imagined life as an open road. Tom's first breakdown happened when they were in their twenties. She couldn't even pretend to know what an open road might feel like. It's up to you now, Polly Osborne instructed at their wedding. *Keep our brilliant boy safe.* Even before Catharine knew all she was being asked, she wanted to cry: And what about me?

She'd failed Polly Osborne's mandate. Tom's parents treated her now with a hint of disapproval. As though it were her fault, those days Tom wouldn't get out of bed, or he did only to wander the house unshaven.

"Tell me about your son," Gavin said.

The question flung her out of time. "Toby." The sound of her son's name grounded her. "He's nothing like me, well, not entirely. Though we've always been close. He doesn't care for poetry."

The waiter filled her water glass and Catharine paused, as though confiding a secret her son wouldn't want her to share. "He builds things," she said at last. "He wants to be an architect. Though, unfortunately, last year he also discovered he hates math."

"And your husband?"

The question surprised her. Catharine wondered what a stranger might see in her smile. "He teaches as well. A community college an hour or so away from where we live."

"And where's that again?"

"Near Boston. Have you been?"

"To the States once, but never Boston." He added, "Disneyland, in fact."

"I can't imagine you in Disneyland."

"When Sinéad's boys were young. Hideous place."

"I hate Mickey Mouse." She laughed.

Gavin raised his glass in agreement.

To her relief, coupled with a fleeting stab of disappointment, at the end of the evening he walked her back to her hotel across from the National Library and they shook hands.

The next morning there was a message waiting when she went down to breakfast. He'd thought about it after they parted, and realized Catharine shouldn't leave Dublin before seeing the bog exhibit across the street from where she was staying. Would she meet him there that afternoon? Join him for dinner?

Catharine was glad to hear his voice again.

"What exactly is a bog?" she asked when she phoned him back. "And why does Ireland have so many of them?"

"Exactly," he replied. "And now, how can you leave without knowing?"

Catharine laughed. "What time then?"

The exhibit snaked through a concrete maze of re-created bog pits, cases of artifacts, mummies preserved by centuries buried beneath sodden ground. One had a leather cord around its neck, the face a grimace frozen in time. The display label explained the man's death by suffocation in peat was an ancient form of human sacrifice.

Others had died in the bogs by accident or been entombed there by choice. Brittle brown garments that looked like lace were preserved under glass, clothing rendered art by long centuries under a mire. Catharine wondered about the people who might have worn them. An unlucky farmer slipping into a ditch, a stumbling drunk on his way home from the pub. An unfaithful wife.

"And now for something cheerier!" Gavin announced as he hailed a taxi once the museum closed. "I've made reservations at the restaurant below the Writers Museum. On her final night in Dublin, a visiting poet needs to dine at Chapter One."

"This is too expensive," Catharine said as soon as she caught a glimpse of the menu at the door.

"It is," he said. "I haven't been here since Sinéad died."

"I should pay half."

"You Americans! So fiercely independent." Gavin refused her offer. "When we meet again, you may do me the honor."

She tried to imagine the circumstances where they'd ever meet again. Gavin Royce transposed to Boston. She couldn't imagine him there. After tonight, she'd never see him again which was, at once, a relief and utterly sad.

"Were you in Dublin during the Troubles?" she asked after the waiter took their menus.

"I was. A terrible time."

All those years, she and Tom in their house by the sea, insulated from the world's turmoil, subject only to Tom's own. "We take so much for granted," she said.

"Chaos ever at the door."

"That's a grim thought."

"It is. Sorry." Gavin delved into the inside pocket of his suit jacket. "I brought you something. A piece of Ireland, a remembrance of your journey." He placed a triangular rock on the table. Layers of crystals shimmered in candlelight. "A paperweight for your work. A gift from an admiring geologist."

Catharine reached for the stone and his hand briefly hovered over hers. Their eyes met. "Did you find this?"

"Long ago. In the Wicklow Mountains. Not far from here. If you had another day, perhaps we'd go."

"I'd have liked that."

After dinner, there was still light in the sky. It wasn't raining. They walked back to her hotel where hours ago, the afternoon had begun. They stood talking beneath the streetlight until Gavin put down his briefcase and held her by the shoulders. "I'm going to miss you, you know."

He circled his arms to pull her close, kissing her full on the lips, not once in farewell as she expected they might, but hungrily, greedily, and Catharine was freed from the restlessness that had gripped her these last days, to realize she didn't feel what she thought she would. No flash of cosmic recognition.

When she and Tom were young, their passion was the bond that kept them whole. Their heads coming to rest beside the night table after making love, the bedside lamp teetering; Catharine falling asleep in the wet spot warmed by their bodies. How comforting that seemed. So long ago.

Gavin's kiss stirred none of that.

She drew back. "This week has been—"

"For me, as well," he added hastily. Then he straightened, his proper bearing returned. He bowed slightly. Catharine extended her hand, and he shook it, then raised it to his lips. "Safe journey, my American poet."

He picked up his briefcase and she watched him walk away. At the corner he turned and called out: "I want to see that book of poetry, Catharine Osborne." He waved once and then he was gone.

Catharine returned to her hotel room and pushed a chair to the window overlooking Kildare Street, watching the blue evening deepen, thinking over their encounter, what had transpired the last three days, thinking of her husband and son across the sea waiting for her return.

Passersby went about their lives on the street below. An old woman leaned into a walker, a laughing couple.

A solitary man in a raincoat approached, then stood beneath the streetlight searching his phone, and she thought for a moment it was him, but it wasn't.

CHAPTER 13

The Key

TOM WAS AGITATED, but in a good way, when Catharine came through the front door the next evening. She was exhausted from her delayed flight from Dublin, the long drive home from Boston. He rushed to meet her in the front hall, his eyes shining, a flash of the old Tom, as though she'd summoned him through last night's memory of their love. "You missed the excitement," he announced.

"What excitement?" She hoped it wouldn't have to do with Toby. It didn't.

"Last night. The girl next door. The girl staying in the rental cottage. A family from Connecticut. She hit a girl in the woods."

"Hit her how?"

"With a car. Ran her over. Toby knows her from school, the girl who got hurt."

"My God." Catharine put down her bags. She realized her husband hadn't said hello. This news was his greeting, presented like an offering, the drama next door taking place while she was across the Atlantic. Both events would forever be linked in memory, a betrayal that didn't happen, the accident that did.

Tom came to stand beside her. He opened his arms and she fell into his familiar embrace. He kissed the top of her head. "I missed you."

Catharine circled her arms around his waist. She couldn't say that she'd missed her husband—she'd been too happy to be on her own, grateful for the respite from her daily life, days where she had nothing to think about besides being the poet she used to be. Whatever had transpired with Gavin. Still, she was relieved to be back, more so than she would have thought.

Tom felt thinner than she remembered. "I'm glad you and Toby are okay." That was all she could manage in her weariness; she hoped it sounded like enough.

"I'm going to crash," she said. "I guess I can say that, now that I'm off a plane."

She saw Tom wince. He didn't like jokes about death. She leaned forward and kissed him on the cheek. "We'll talk tomorrow. And I bring gifts! Irish tea, chocolates! I found a great Book of Kells T-shirt for Toby."

Tom pulled her close once more. He hugged her tightly. "Last night was surreal," he said. "It made me think—" He hesitated. "About a lot of things."

"Do you want me to stay up a while longer?" she forced herself to offer. "We can talk now."

"No, no, not now. I can see you're exhausted."

"Tomorrow," she promised.

Tom released his hold and turned back to the kitchen. "I'm glad you're back."

"Me, too," Catharine added a beat later than she'd intended.

She woke before dawn the next morning, sleepless, hoping to resist the resumption of her daily life a few hours longer. She didn't want to think about what was for dinner. About having to go to the grocery store, or her suitcase of laundry. She wanted to linger for a few more hours in Dublin, drifting down Nassau Street past the brick walls of Trinity, wandering through the campus. Listening to people's accents. Her unexpected encounter with Gavin. She watched Tom asleep in the early blue light, oblivious to her presence. She quietly shut the door to the bedroom and went downstairs.

Out in the garden, the hydrangeas were in full bloom, falling over themselves beside the porch, the black-eyed Susans just opening up. Waves crashed against rocks, reverberating from the nearby cove. She smelled seaweed and salt air. High tide. She took a sip of her tea.

What would Gavin be doing in Dublin at lunchtime? She pictured him striding through campus and remembered the shining pyramid rock he'd presented her on their last evening. Its beauty didn't belong on a desk. It needed a garden.

Catharine tiptoed inside to retrieve the stone. In the sunlight, the intricate patterns of pink and white crystals glittered as they had beneath candlelight. She felt again the warmth of his hand above hers.

What did she feel, truly feel, if she let herself? Part of her did wish a life with Gavin Royce could have been possible. An alternate future where she'd be free of Tom, even as she knew she'd never be free of him. Neither could she betray him. She hadn't. Catharine thought that was true. A single kiss wasn't a betrayal. Was it?

Kneeling above the flower bed, she saw the weeds starting to take over. Somehow, the winter never managed to kill what grew wild.

The porch door opened, and Tom stepped outside with a cup of coffee. He squinted and took off his glasses. In flannel pajama bottoms and a T-shirt, he looked almost boyish in the light. Catharine was glad, deeply glad, that nothing more had happened.

"There you are," Tom said. "I've been looking all over for you."

"Here I am."

She left Gavin's stone in the flower bed and followed Tom inside to the kitchen. "How was it?" he turned to ask.

The last ten days passed before Catharine's mind, her happiness to finally be in Ireland on her own, the disappointment of Archie Dent and his workshop. Gavin.

"You were right about Archie Dent," Catharine told him, recalling Tom's disdain for the man the day they first met. "He is a prick."

"I told you." Tom nodded. "But you got what you were looking for?"

"I think so."

When Catharine went upstairs later, she found him in his study, gesturing wildly toward the window as though conducting an orchestra, talking to himself. Composing a new poem? How many years had it been since he'd written anything. Maybe reciting one from memory, though it didn't sound like he was doing either. Catharine backed out of the doorway.

Tom heard the floorboards creak and turned to find her there.

"Do you hate me?" he asked suddenly. The boyishness she'd glimpsed earlier was gone. He looked drained of color in the window's light.

"Of course I don't hate you."

"I wouldn't blame you if you did."

"Tom—," she said with tenderness, though inwardly she wanted to cry. Was it too much to hope to prolong her brief escape a few more hours before being sucked back into Tom's world? She felt profoundly tired of her role keeping Polly's brilliant boy safe. He was forty-eight years old. Hadn't she done enough? He could look out for himself finally, couldn't he?

No, he couldn't.

And it came to her, as it had earlier, how deeply she wished it had been possible to fall in love with someone else. To forget about Tom. Though, of course, she'd never forget, never stop caring what happened to him. Was that love? Is that what love was? She didn't know anymore. But yes, part of her wished it was Gavin Royce she'd been waiting for all those years.

"I did some thinking while you were gone," Tom said.

"I did too."

"I'm sorry I never gave you what you wanted."

"That's not true."

"Isn't it?"

"Oh, Tom," Catharine said. "Let's not do this now."

"Then when?"

"I'm exhausted," she said.

"You just woke up."

Catharine said nothing. They faced each other across the room in silence until Tom finally shook his head. "Okay, right. I get it. I'm an idiot. You need to settle in."

"You're not an idiot."

"Sometimes I am."

Catharine sighed. "I'm going to take a shower."

"Watch out for the shower faucet. It's doing that thing again where it sprays water all over the ceiling."

Catharine managed to laugh. "Of course it is."

Catharine's parents were not pleased when she told them she was marrying Tom Osborne, a man they'd never met. No ring, of course. That would have been bourgeois then.

She'd taken the train down from Boston to break the news. Her parents were behind the counter after the deli closed, prepping for the next day, her mother in her apron, Catharine's father in a white T-shirt and black docksiders, his daily uniform. Catharine sat on the same stool she'd occupied as a child when her father served her egg cream sodas. Now his open pack of Winstons rested beside the metal napkin dispenser.

Catharine's cousin Buddy stood with his back turned, slicing roast beef. As though a silent agreement had passed between them, Buddy turned off the slicer, wiped his hands and grabbed his jacket, heading for the door. Her parents turned as one to face her.

"Married, Kit-Cat?" her mother began. "I know there's the baby, and you think you have no choice, but have you really thought this out?"

Catharine had. She felt protective of the new life inside her in a way she could never explain, certainly not to the stony faces of her parents confronting her across the counter of the deli. Amaretto cookies and Charles Chips, the refrigerator case of cold cuts and salads, the stack of *Newsdays* by the register. Her decision had been sealed by a dream in which she made a different choice. That couldn't be what they wanted, too? Not her father. Jimmy Conor, the altar boy.

"A baby, Kitty?" he asked. "Do you know what that means? To take care of a baby. Your life will be over."

"How can you say that?"

"Something's changed in you since you met this Tom. All you talk about is Tom. Tom said this, Tom thinks that. Tom, Tom, Tom. Do you realize that?"

"I'm in love with him."

"Do you even know him?" her mother spoke up. "What's it been, how many months?"

"Long enough to fall in love with him."

"Oh, Catharine."

"What?"

"For a smart girl, you're so naïve."

"He writes poetry?" her father scoffed. "That's going to support a family?"

"He doesn't have to support me. I have a scholarship."

"What does that pay, Kitty? You could be helping out at the deli and make more than you earn from a scholarship."

"I'm going to finish college. I don't want to work at the deli."

"No, you're too good for that. You and the poet."

"Why do you have to be like this?" Catharine pleaded, tears in her eyes.

"Your mother just wants you to be happy," her father said.

"Then let me be happy!" Catharine said.

"Kitty," her mother sighed, "we don't understand you anymore. I wonder if we ever did."

Her father died the winter she and Tom returned from England. An aneurysm at the store. Tom drove her back to Queens in the middle of the night and stayed at a Super 8 motel near the Whitestone Bridge. He never saw her mother after the funeral, which was Rachel Conor's choice. "It's all too much right now, baby. I'm not myself." She never was again.

She died of heart failure a year later.

The first Sunday afterwards when Catharine returned from New York for dinner at the Osbornes', Polly pecked her cheek. "Think of us as your parents now."

She managed to choke out thanks.

"Tom will tell you," Polly assured her, "I always wished he'd been a daughter."

Toby was in the kitchen when Catharine came downstairs after her shower. "Mom!" He jumped up from his bowl of cereal, pulling her into a hug. Catharine felt the strength of his arms. He'd been lifting weights in his bedroom at night, the clunk of metal hitting the ceiling above the dining room after he was done. "He's going to put a crack in that ceiling," Tom always warned.

Toby seldom hugged her that way anymore. Catharine was happy to think he'd missed her, too. Her miracle son, the surprise after they'd given up, the baby who lived. "Did Dad tell you what happened?" was the first thing he said.

"The girl staying next door? He told me, but I don't think I get it. She was arrested?"

"She ran over somebody in the woods. Gabriela Ortiz. She goes to my school. Her mother cleans the cottage next door."

"Her mother is the woman who cleans next door?"

At her attic desk, Catharine had occasionally seen a woman hauling vacuum and buckets from the trunk of an old car. She'd notice her shaking out throw rugs, emptying garbage, the sounds of the vacuum and washing machine a low hum through the open windows after renters left.

"Her father's a landscaper in town," Toby said.

Catharine pictured the battered girl in a hospital bed, the careless one from Connecticut who'd likely go free; immigrant men with gas tanks strapped to their backs, mowing summer people's lawns. "Is the girl okay?" Catharine asked.

"No. Mom. She was hit by a car."

Catharine shook her head. "Sorry. I'm not entirely here yet."

"Me neither." Toby laughed. "Sorry, I didn't even ask about your trip yet. Was it great? How was Ireland?"

"Green. Just like they say."

"And?" Toby rolled his eyes. He never let her get away with easy answers.

"I learned some things," Catharine said.

"About *la poésie*?" Her son spoofed her in the mock accent that always made her laugh.

She smiled. "Poetry and life, my son."

"I thought poetry *was* life."

She loved this jocular side of him, the teasing relationship they'd always shared. Toby kept more to himself, now that he was fifteen. A silent deep thinker, Tom without the darkness. He was starting to resemble him, too, elusively conjuring the Tom she'd fallen in love with that summer in Cambridge. The shape of his face, the same furrowed eyebrows, serious eyes. Would her son confide in her if he ever began to experience the turmoil

Tom did when he was young? She longed to let him know, as
she used to when he was younger: "You can always talk to me,
Toby. You know you can, right?" But she couldn't bring herself
to say those words. How would he process that unexplained
intrusion of her concern?

Sometimes she wished they could go back to the time when
Toby was a boy and he'd sit beside her at the table, sketching
out inventions while she reworked stanzas. She worried that
maybe she didn't pay enough attention to him then. He seemed
so self-reliant. She valued her precious stolen writing hours too
much. And yet, he'd turned out okay. He'd always been okay.
How easily he'd made friends with that boy next door the summer his family rented the cottage. They even invited Toby out
on their fancy boat. He was a great kid. Everyone said so. When
she tried to imagine Tom at fifteen, she couldn't.

"Hey, guess what I did while you were gone?"

"Don't know."

"I got a job," Toby said.

"A job! Where?"

"The Fish Hut in town."

"Doing what?"

"Dishwasher."

Catharine laughed. "Have you actually ever washed a dish?
I can't remember."

"I've washed dishes!" Toby protested. "I started last week."

"Do you like it?"

"It's okay. I like earning money."

"There you go."

"I've got something to show you, by the way. Come down to
the basement later. See what I built for Dad's birthday."

Catharine remembered Tom struggling to construct a cradle down there after her second miscarriage. The mess of tools and cups and dishes, nails scattered everywhere, hammered pieces of wood kicked over on the floor, the frenzy of his woodworking effort in the days before he checked himself in to McLean.

That afternoon after work, Toby showed her his creation, a sturdy, well-crafted bookcase. She had no idea her teenage son could build anything like that. "This is great, Toby. All that woodworking detail." Catharine shook her head in astonishment. "How did you learn to build a bookcase?"

"Shop class."

"Really?"

Toby laughed. "What did you think we do in shop class?"

"Work on cars?"

"Right." Toby grinned.

Catharine ran a hand over the bookcase's polished surface, hoping Tom would be as astonished by the gift as she was, that he would be able to convey that to his son. As though he'd read her mind, Toby asked, "Do you think Dad's okay?"

"How do you mean?"

"You know. Does he seem okay to you?" He busied himself returning hammer and nails to the toolbox. When he glanced up to meet Catharine's eyes, she saw the worry there.

"Did anything happen while I was gone?"

"No," Toby hurried to say. "Well, the stuff next door. Nothing, I guess. I don't know what I meant about Dad. It's hard to explain. Maybe just that he's deep in himself. More than he usually is."

Catharine longed to tell him what she really felt. No, she didn't think Tom was okay. As always, she felt torn. The fine balance between saying too much and too little, wanting to shield their son from Tom's illness, to spare Toby the sorrows he didn't yet need to bear. Probably he'd known for a long time that Tom was not like other fathers, but they never spoke the words. Toby was old enough now, but Catharine was not anxious to have that conversation. Not today. Another time, soon. Or—could she hope?—maybe what she'd glimpsed in Tom that morning would pass, another bout of darkness. Maybe they could go on, as they always had. They always had.

"You don't have to worry about Dad," she offered at last. "He's probably just tired from being a single parent all week. I bet he'll be glad not to have to cook dinner tonight."

"Dad loves to cook."

This was true. He did love to cook, he always had. An amateur gourmet chef, admired by their friends.

"Anyway, I helped while you were gone," Toby told her. "I even cooked myself one night."

"What did you make?"

"Burgers. On the grill."

Catharine wondered which day that was. A night when she'd had dinner with Gavin Royce? She pictured an alternate homecoming if things had gone differently. Her son in the same jeans and T-shirt, proudly showing off his handcraft while she'd be standing there, trying to formulate a confession: "I have something to tell you, Toby. I met someone while I was in Ireland," she imagined saying. "Your father and I are getting a divorce."

She erased the mental picture of her son trying to take in that new reality, grief and confusion in his eyes. Or Tom's. She couldn't fathom saying those words to Tom. She was grateful not to have to.

It was late afternoon when she finally returned to the task she left behind when Tom appeared at the door. She returned to the solace of her garden to find the right spot for Gavin's gift. The air was different outside. She could breathe.

She worked her hands into the soil to free the stifling weeds. Digging a little deeper, her gloved hands closed around something hard. She brushed away the earth and saw what she held was a car key, the old-fashioned kind, attached to a tarnished good luck charm. She suddenly knew who it belonged to.

Emma's son. Once, Emma Nolan knelt in this spot and buried those keys in the ground.

The key chain must have belonged to Kyle, her youngest, dead in a waterskiing accident the summer he turned eighteen. When Catharine overheard this at Emma's memorial, she understood the full meaning of the words the older woman spoke that day in Boston.

Sometimes they'll break your heart.

For a minute, Catharine knelt there, not knowing what to do. Clean off this relic, find a home for those keys and their good luck charm inside her house, a talisman, but of what? Nothing good. Toby was practically Kyle's age now.

Quickly, she patted the metal back into the ground where she'd uncovered it, wishing she'd never done so, the spot Emma Nolan once chose for this remnant of her son. She marked the place beneath the lilac with Gavin's pyramid stone. She made a wish.

Catharine prayed that whatever wrecked Tom and his father before him would never touch their son.

CHAPTER 14

Lives of the Saints

"I'VE INVITED THE ROSENS for dinner this weekend," Tom told her that night. "I know you're just back. Is that okay?"

"Of course."

Syd and Jessie Rosen were colleagues of Tom's from the college. Tom had initiated an invitation, which seemed to dispel what frightened her earlier that morning when she came upon him talking to himself. He must be all right if he wanted to have people for dinner.

In company, her husband could be a different person. Catharine always marveled at the transformation. Their friends didn't know the depths he could sink to, this man presiding over a feast with robust good humor. In the kitchen, seated around the dinner table after a meal he'd prepared, Tom always seemed his best self—the gifted, laughing man he sometimes still was.

Their friends had no idea of his history. They thought teaching at a community college in a rough part of the city made him a saint, instead of being the only job his father could find for him despite Tom's advanced degrees. He'd been expelled from Harvard; he had a criminal record. One of Tom's friends actually did tell Catharine she'd married "a saint" after a few drinks once at a party. Helping those deserving kids. Didn't the Osbornes always give of themselves? Tom's mother and her committees. Dr. Osborne had a park named after him in Ravenna.

Tom chose to cook paella for the Rosens' dinner, an elaborate dish that was reliably one of his triumphs. He'd gone to the fish market in nearby New Vernon that afternoon and bought the catch straight off the boat as he always did, then spent the rest of the day in the kitchen.

That night, after the plates were cleared, Syd Rosen spoke up. "So, Tom," he said. "What's this I hear you're not going to apply for Dan's job?"

Catharine looked at Tom, but he was pouring more wine. "The chairmanship?" she asked.

Syd turned to her. "McAllen's retiring. Tom didn't tell you?"

"I've been in Ireland."

"Oh right!" Jessie Rosen turned to Catharine. "Lucky you. How was it?"

"Wonderful," Catharine replied without thinking. She was looking at Tom, but he wouldn't glance in her direction.

"That job needs a good manager," Tom said. "I'm not a manager."

"But you're well liked," Syd pointed out.

Tom tried to joke. "Which I'd like to remain."

After a few minutes rehashing the same points in different words, Catharine noticed Jessie lay a hand on Syd's arm and he let the topic drop.

Catharine brought it up again when they were washing dishes later, their guests having departed back to the city. "You're really not going to apply?"

Her husband's pained expression told her he wasn't. "It's not for me, Cat. I can't do that kind of job. Who would want that level of pressure?"

"Is it that much pressure?" she asked.

Tom turned to face her. "Look, teaching I can do. Managing other people? Dealing with their personalities and budgets and the politics of it all? No, never. That's not me. I can't do it."

"I think you could."

"You're wrong," was all he said.

Was even an opportunity in Tom's path beyond him now? The brilliant boy who never was, the man who might have been. Catharine refused to accept he'd given up. She kept on, urging him to reconsider until he covered his face with his hands. "What do you want from me, Catharine? I can't do it, okay? I can't."

"It's more money," she said despite herself, hating that she said it. "We could finally fix the kitchen."

The kitchen or any of the other myriad things that needed fixing and had for years. The endearing yet aggravating gouge in the living room floor etched by Toby's ice skates long ago; the loose slab of crown molding that bobbed up and down like an open-mouth beast on the ceiling whenever a door slammed.

They could pay a handyman to do these things if only the money wasn't always needed somewhere else. Tom's medical expenses not covered by insurance, his drugs with three-figure co-pays. Toby's braces, summer camp, the furnace that died one January and had to be replaced. It wasn't that they were poor. They weren't poor, they were privileged people, continually scrambling to hold on to their crumbling perch within the diminishing middle class.

"I'm sorry I brought up the kitchen," Catharine said at last to change the mood.

He stared at her mutely. "I don't care about the kitchen."

"What do you care about, Tom?"

He looked shocked by the question, as though he'd never considered it before. "You, of course. Toby. Our life together." He was quiet for a time, thinking, before his expression darkened. "Maybe nothing?"

CHAPTER 15

Veritas

ON HOT SUMMER NIGHTS, Toby liked to take the long way home after waiting tables at the Fish Hut. He'd pedal out to Quail Beach where he'd swum ashore the day he fled Jake's boat. A quick plunge to rinse off the smells of seafood and ketchup was a ritual that restored him.

He was at work, surveying the dining room from his corner near the busboy station, the night he first saw the girl from Quail Beach again. It was the Friday after Thanksgiving in what would have been his freshman year in college. People-watching between orders was one of the perks of waiting tables, a habit Toby inherited from his mother, inventing stories about strangers.

The Fish Hut was a popular spot for tourists and townies alike. Faux nautical crab claws and netting adorned the walls, décor that could have been any coastal restaurant from Florida to Maine. Toby was taking a gap year that fall. His father had died a few months before, and his mother needed his company, at least for a while. He was working at the restaurant, living at home. Left unsaid was the real reason he didn't consider going away to school. The insurance company was giving his mother a hard time, and they couldn't afford it.

Three days a week, Toby took a few free courses at the community college in the city where his dad taught. His mother cried when she opened the dean's letter. Free tuition, just as though his father hadn't died but was still alive, still on the faculty. The commute was long—a train ride into Boston, followed by two subways, but worth it to build up credits to transfer somewhere else, someday. That was the plan. He knew he had to leave Belle Harbor. Get on with his life. He would one day. In the meantime, his mother needed him. At least for a while.

Scanning the dining room that Thanksgiving weekend, Toby recognized a girl seated in his section at a table of returning college kids. He couldn't figure out how he knew her. She hadn't gone to Belle Harbor high school, though the friends she was sitting with had. Her long, blonde hair was almost white; translucent skin, all of her pale except for her startling eyes that matched her turquoise sweater. Her eyes were what he recognized.

Toby snuck glances when she wasn't looking. The first time their gaze met, she seemed to acknowledge him, too. He hadn't approached their table yet, hadn't gotten to the part he hated: "Hi, my name is Toby and I'll be taking care of you tonight."

When he did, the girl looked up. Her face was covered in light freckles. "Hey, is that you?" she asked right away.

"Who?" Toby still couldn't place her.

"The Swimmer." She smiled as though they already shared the joke. "That's what we always called you. My mom and my sister. We saw you that day. We were out on the beach the afternoon you appeared out of the waves like—I don't know—the Creature from the Deep. That was so wild. I've always wondered what you were doing way out there."

"What was I doing?" Toby laughed. "I was swimming."

"I know, but from where? Did you swim all the way from that boat beyond the breakwater? My mom said you did."

Toby nodded. "Yeah."

"Why would you do that?"

"I don't know. I had to."

The girl agreed. "That's what I always thought, too."

Toby took their order and watched from the kitchen as the girl and her friends returned to their laughter. Once his section filled, he couldn't get back to their table. Another waiter brought their food and the check. When Toby went to process the bill, he saw she'd written her phone number on a napkin. The girl from Quail Beach had a name, Megan Foley.

He phoned her the next day, rode his bike down to the cove so his mother wouldn't hear. He composed the message he'd leave if he got her voicemail, but she picked up on the third ring. The raw November wind made it impossible to hear. He clamped a gloved hand to his ear.

"Hey, it's Toby," he said. "From the restaurant."

"Toby, who took care of us last night!" she teased in a mischievous voice.

"I know. Don't you hate that? I hate that they make us say that stuff."

"I'm glad you called," Megan said.

Two gulls shrieked overhead, fighting over something one of them clutched in its beak. "Is that a seagull?" the girl asked.

"Yep."

"Where are you?"

"I'm out on Flat Rock."

"Where's that?"

"Down the road from my house."

"Hey, want to go for a walk on the beach where we met?" Her tone sounded familiar, as though they were old friends.

"Sure." Toby watched a family of ducks bob along the cove. "Now?"

"In a half hour."

She was already walking the beach at Quail Point when he arrived, in a purple down jacket and mittens, her blonde hair loose beneath a wool hat pulled low over her forehead. Toby was wearing the gray, crimson-lettered sweatshirt that had been his father's.

"Aren't you cold?" was the first thing she said. The second was: "You go to Harvard?"

Toby shook his head. "I don't get cold."

"You don't get cold?" Megan laughed.

"I know, it's weird."

"I'm always cold," she said.

"I hope you picked someplace warm for college then."

"Middlebury."

"Vermont!" Toby executed a comic 360-degree turn. "Vermont?"

"I know."

He felt as though he already knew her. "You switched schools." The words came out as a question.

"We moved after fifth grade," Megan answered. "We're back visiting my aunt."

They walked side by side, facing into the wind. "You know that day we watched you swim ashore, I didn't realize until my mom told me later, how far you'd come." Megan gestured beyond the breakers. "I mean, that was huge for a kid."

"I know you didn't see how far it was. You were asleep on the beach. Your mother was the only one watching."

"I wasn't asleep!" Megan protested with mock indignation. "I was tanning."

"Tanning!" Toby laughed. "You know that's unhealthy right?"

"Yes, Dad."

"Just saying." Toby bent to retrieve a stone from the shore and skimmed it across the water. "How old is your little sister now?"

"Fifteen."

"So that day would have been when—seven summers ago?" A scent of lemon shampoo clung to the wind. "I always wanted brothers and sisters," Toby confessed, though he didn't know why he was telling her this.

The girl turned to him. "You're an only child?"

"Can you tell?"

His mother the part-time poet, his father struggling for reasons Toby never understood. He tried to imagine either of them presiding over a house full of siblings, but he never could.

"You want to know the truth?" Megan said. "I always kind of wished I didn't have a sister."

The tendrils of her hair brushed his cheek in the wind. She gathered the loose strands to tuck beneath her cap. "So you're at Harvard?" she asked a second time.

"What?"

"You go to Harvard."

Toby realized he'd grabbed the old crimson logo sweatshirt that still hung where his dad had left it, on a peg by the back door. "No. This was my dad's. I'm waiting a year. I'm taking a 'gap year,'" he added in air quotes. The carefree defense he'd perfected since graduation ended with a shrug, and the hope the topic did, too.

"A lot of kids do that," she said.

Toby took a breath and plunged on. "My father committed suicide this summer."

"What? He did? I mean—that's awful. I'm so sorry."

Toby couldn't believe he'd just blurted those words out to a stranger. A picture he struggled hard to erase from his mind returned, though it was a scene he'd only heard described, his father's body clad in pajamas, floating in the inlet at the end of their street. The police said he'd folded his bathrobe on the ledge beside his phone, taken off his shoes. He didn't leave a note.

The fact that he'd removed his shoes and folded his bathrobe were the details the town chorus seized on to decide his father's death was premeditated. The unbearable week when his father's drowning and the ensuing rumors dominated the local gossip sites confirmed Toby's sense that most people were basically assholes.

Megan touched his arm. "I am so sorry," she said again.

"Don't be sorry. That's the last thing my dad would have wanted. Really."

"But it's awful."

"It is, but it's also kind of unreal, you know? I think about him all the time. Maybe what I feel now will never go away—but then: there's nothing I can do about it either, right? I'm still here. I still love what I always have, and that's all here, too. The ocean. I love the ocean; I love to swim, the woods. My mom. I love my mom. It's not all dark. And then, some days—"

"How did he—?"

"Drowned," Toby said. "Pills. Maybe he didn't mean to. My mother can't talk about it. But I think he did."

"Is she okay?"

Toby didn't want to talk about his mother either. "Let's talk about something else."

"I shouldn't have asked."

Toby thought about reaching over to hold Megan's hand as they tramped the beach side by side, but instead he angled his shoulder close to hers as they continued. "It's fine. A lot of people can't even bring themselves to ask. They don't want to know about it. They don't even want to see me. I'll be in a store and see someone I recognize, and they find something else to look at. I pass them in the aisle and they're staring at the candy rack."

"I'm sorry," she said again.

"You don't have to be sorry."

They stopped walking and looked into each other's eyes. Toby wondered if he should, but then he leaned forward and Megan did the same, and their lips brushed in a brief kiss. She smiled and he kissed her again. "Listen, do you want to go get ice cream?"

"In November?" She laughed. "Sure."

That night he lay in his single bed in the room he'd had since boyhood. It was late fall, still a lingering off-season guest in the rental cottage next door, the cottage his mother hated for the weekly disruption of their quiet lives. He remembered trying to fall asleep as a child with the smell of cigarette smoke drifting through the open window, raised voices of vacationers who'd had too much to drink pealing from the deck, beer bottles crashing into the recycling bin at midnight, his parents arguing in the morning. "I'm going to call the owners," his mother would threaten, to which his father always replied, "The owners are in Florida. What are they going to do?"

Sometimes his parents squabbling was worse, especially those arguments overheard when they didn't know he was listening. Once, Toby was stacking lawn chairs in the shed after one of his parents' summer parties. Their college friends had driven up from the city. After they'd left, his mother seemed upset for reasons Toby didn't understand. He'd heard the words "Harvard" and "fire," and then a door slammed, and he couldn't hear any more. His mother made it sound as though his father had done something terrible before Toby was born. Toby wanted to know what that was, but also he didn't.

His mother was at the kitchen table when he came downstairs the next morning. It surprised him how easily he'd spoken those words to Megan the day before. *My father committed suicide.* Toby had never confessed this to anyone. His mother had never spoken of it. Toby had tried to broach the topic early on, in one of their truncated conversations that summer.

"I can't think about that now," she'd said. "I can't, Toby. Later, maybe. I just need to get through this week."

But the weeks went on and they never spoke of it. Toby wanted to raise the subject, but he feared he'd only upset her. He wanted to know what she thought really happened—did he intend to drown? was it an accident?

His mother was sipping tea, staring out the sliding glass door off the kitchen as he came down the stairs.

"Was Dad fired from Harvard?" he asked when he saw her look up.

She turned to face him. "What did you say?"

"Did Dad teach at Harvard and get fired?"

"No. Never." She seemed pale in the sunlight. "What made you ask that?"

"I was thinking about something last night. About a time I heard you talking after a party, after everybody left."

She didn't answer right away. He could tell she was trying to decide something. "How long have you wondered about that? Harvard, being fired."

"A long time. Ever since I overheard you arguing that day. I was pretty young."

"You heard us arguing?" She looked down.

"I didn't mean to listen."

"It's all right. I guess there's no point in keeping secrets any-more, is there?" She laughed, but not in a good way. Toby leaned against the wall, wishing now he hadn't asked. His mother took a sip of tea and set the cup down on its china saucer. "Dad was a student at Harvard. He was in grad school when we met."

"Right, I know that."

His mother hesitated. "The part you don't know is why he had to leave. When I tell you what he did, Toby, you have to promise to remember sometimes he wasn't well."

"What did he do?"

"It was a bad time."

"Mom. Just tell me. What did he do?"

"He set a fire at the library. That was the fire you heard us talk about. He wasn't fired. *He set a fire.*"

Toby tried to fathom his quiet father doing such a thing, a man who cherished learning, who loved books, a father who regularly reprimanded Toby for the sin of cracking the spines of those he left face-down on the couch.

"He set fire to a *library*? At Harvard?"

"A small fire." His mother hastened to add. "A few books in the stacks. They put it out in five minutes. No one was hurt. It's not as though he wanted to burn down the building!" She tried to sound lighthearted, but her tight smile gave her away.

"Why would he do that?"

"He was ill, Toby. You know that. He didn't like to talk about it, but sometimes …" She hesitated. "Sometimes he wasn't himself. You know that. You do."

"I know."

He remembered the panic in his mother's eyes that afternoon at the Christmas Revels. When she'd addressed him on one knee with that intent look she seldom had now: *Toby, tell me really, was that fun?* He didn't know how to answer; he'd said that it was.

Riding high above the crowd on his father's shoulders moments before, the two of them galloping through the lobby with the cast, all of them singing "Lord of the Dance," Toby had felt like a king buoyed by the actors' resounding voices: *Dance, then! Wherever you may be!* But he was scared, too, and this he would never confess to his mother. His father's grip on Toby's little legs seemed to slip in time with the music.

Or the summer years ago when they'd gone for ice cream and his father insisted that the girl behind the window provide samples of every flavor. Toby sensed the irritation growing behind them in the line, but his father took no notice until Toby tugged at his pocket. "Dad! You should pick one. Butter pecan, you like that, right?"

When his father turned from the counter and looked down, it was as though his eyes focused elsewhere, not yet taking Toby for his son. "Sorry for that," he said to the server. "Two cones. Butter pecan and chocolate." Toby's father pushed a ten-dollar bill toward the window. "I don't need change."

"He was on new meds," his mother was saying now. "We thought they were working—I don't know, maybe they were."

Her words drifted off. She glanced up with the vacant expression that came over her now since June. A remoteness that was new. It was grief, but maybe she was on medication, too. His mother was there, but she wasn't.

"The last few months—" She hesitated. "It was happening again. Like being pulled into a cave. The earth opens and you're just sucked down. That's how he described it." She shook her head. "How did we start talking about this?"

"Harvard."

"Right." His mother looked away. Toby waited for her to go on.

After a while, she picked up her pen. The discussion was over, the window into his parents' lives quietly closing, leaving him once more deciphering clues. When she turned to him again, she seemed lighter. "It's Thanksgiving weekend," she said. "You must have friends who are home. You should go out tonight."

His mother was always urging him to go places, as though Belle Harbor had any place he wanted to go. "Actually, I do have a date later," Toby said, happy to cheer her.

Her face brightened. "A date! With whom?"

"A girl you don't know. She's visiting for Thanksgiving. Megan Foley."

"Megan Foley? I don't know that name."

"See!" Toby laughed. "I told you that you wouldn't."

"How do you know her?"

"From the restaurant."

"She works there?"

"No, Mom. She's visiting. For Thanksgiving."

"Right. You said that. Do you want to eat something before you go? There are leftovers."

Toby's mother had roused herself to roast a turkey breast on Thanksgiving, though she seldom cooked anymore.

"No, I'm good. I think I'm going to take a bath actually."

"A bath!" His mother laughed in a way she hadn't in a long time.

"I like baths."

"Since when?" She didn't wait for an answer. "Getting turned out for his date! Mr. November!" she teased as he passed behind her on his way up the stairs.

His mother used to make jokes like that when his dad was alive. Toby felt the same flickering hope he'd had before, that maybe she'd be herself again one day, his mother the way she used to be, when his father was alive.

Toby had begun taking baths in the guest room tub that fall once the weather turned cool. He felt comfort staring at the same ceiling his father had, the crack in the plaster from the year before, the ceiling his father kept promising to fix, asking Toby if he'd help. Toby always said he would, though the crack never got fixed.

One night last spring, his father had passed out in the tub. Water overflowed into the hallway as Toby's mother stood shouting through the door, jiggling the locked handle. "Tom. Tom! What are you doing in there? Tom!"

That was April. By summer, he was dead.

All that warm evening, they'd heard the Coast Guard helicopter crisscrossing the inlet at the end of their street, searchlights scanning the dusk. His mother was at her chair, writing in one of her notebooks when Toby came downstairs to make a sandwich.

"I hate the sound of that helicopter." She lifted her head. "Another diver. Every summer, another drowning. Lately, it seems every year."

Toby remembered the summer the unlucky snorkeler had been part of a Quebec group that rented the cottage. "You know I heard them having sex," Toby told his mom. "That couple from Quebec. The diver who died."

"You heard them having sex?"

"They were in a tent, not far from my window."

His mother laughed. "I think they had fifteen people staying there that week. One bathroom! How old were you then?"

"I don't know, thirteen? I thought it was raccoons. I did at first."

Toby would always remember that was the last conversation they had before the cop knocked on the door. He and his mother were still in the kitchen when the helicopter shut off its searchlight a while earlier, but they hadn't noticed. His mother tried to argue with the young cop who told her the news.

"But he's in bed upstairs. He's reading a book." Neither Toby nor his mother had been aware that his father had gone out.

"I'm sorry, ma'am." The young officer looked contrite, as though it were his fault. Toby ran up the back stairs to check.

"He's not there, Mom," he reported, flush with the news.

"He has to be there." She was insistent.

The two policemen stood in the door. Toby recognized one of them as the cop who was always breaking up teen parties in the woods. "A neighbor spotted him in the cove," the apologetic one said. "She called 911. We found his bathrobe, and his phone."

"He's in the house," his mother said more forcefully, and for a moment, Toby wavered, wanting to believe she knew something he didn't. His father was still alive, playing a game, hiding.

Toby stared again at the fissure above the tub. Why had he and his father never patched it all those months they talked about it? He should do something now. He would next week when he had a day off.

For today, he had a party to go to with Megan. Toby couldn't remember the last time he'd looked forward to anything. He slid beneath the water, and his hair floated around him like seaweed. He hadn't had a haircut since May. Beneath the surface, Toby held his breath. On swim team, he was always the one to hold his breath the longest, one minute, two minutes. And then a little more.

Viewed from the tub's bottom, the bathroom light shone from another world; wallpaper shimmered green. He heard the muffled sound of a radio playing downstairs and thought again of the strangeness of the song his mother chose for his father's memorial. Jackson Browne's "Something Fine," with its mysterious line about Morocco. Had his parents ever been to Morocco? If they had, they never spoke of it. Underwater, holding his breath, Toby saw the truth emerge as clearly as if someone whispered it to him.

It was an accident.

He opened his eyes, sat up, and took a breath. His eyes stung. An initiate awoken from a rite. His father hadn't drowned on purpose. He didn't kill himself.

Wrapped in a towel, Toby stood before the medicine cabinet, dripping water on the floor, and he saw they were still there, a half-dozen amber vials, his father's pills. Toby examined the labels, the same CVS bottles his father once held. He read the warnings. *May cause drowsiness, dizziness, blackouts.*

It was an accident.

His father would have left a note if he'd meant to kill himself. Of course he would have. Speaking the words out loud to

Megan as they walked the beach, acknowledging his father's suicide, made those words seem no longer true. The message boards had it wrong. They didn't know his father.

Toby found his mother downstairs, still working on one of her notebooks in the kitchen. "Dad didn't kill himself!" he announced, a marathon runner delivering his news.

"I know," she said.

"You know?"

His mother turned and gazed at him with her full attention.

"Why would he do that to us?" she asked.

Toby nodded. "He wouldn't."

Is that what she believed, too? Or was she shielding him now as she always had, a boy growing up within his parents' silences.

"Come here, sweetheart."

His mother extended a hand, and he went to where she sat beneath the kitchen light. Toby waited for her to say something more, but she didn't. She hugged him close.

Toby bent to kiss the top of her head. Her hair smelled like childhood.

CHAPTER 16

Local Hero

THE DAY HE WALKED out on his shift waiting tables at the Fish Hut, Toby didn't know he'd never return. The dining room manager was a friend, and Toby figured he could talk his way back on the schedule. They were always short-handed.

It was late summer, the end of tourist season, his afternoon shift almost over when he spotted Phil and Marcie Rhibek seated in his section. Toby remembered them from his father's wake the previous summer. They'd stood at the back of the funeral home, conferring in hushed voices. Maybe they thought he couldn't hear them.

"A closed casket," Mrs. Rhibek pronounced in a knowing voice.

"He was in the water, Marcie," her husband pointed out.

"Not that long, though, was he?"

"Long enough. You know what water does to a body."

"I thought they found him the same day—?"

Toby didn't listen to the rest. He'd returned to his seat beside his mother at the front of the room, bestowing the plastic cup of water he'd brought her. She smiled and took a sip, then continued to stare straight ahead at the polished wood casket beneath the blanket of white roses Toby's grandparents bought.

He'd avoided the Rhibeks for the remainder of that afternoon at the wake, but here they were, eager to be waited on: Mr. Rhibek in a nylon shirt that hugged his nipples, sunglasses on a chain, his wife in a tube top and shorts.

"Toby, son, how are you doing?" Mr. Rhibek greeted him loudly.

"I'm okay," Toby said.

"Must have been tough, losing your dad like that last summer."

"It was."

The upturned face of Marcie Rhibek gazed at him expectantly, phone in hand, ready to post whatever detail about his father's drowning they managed to pry from him in the hour he'd be their server.

Toby got as far as bringing their drinks. When he set the gin and tonic in front of Mrs. Rhibek, she swept him with a somber feint of sympathy. "All these months later, and they never found a note?"

"What did you say?"

Mr. Rhibek handed Toby the drink menus. "I'm a father myself. It seems sad he wouldn't leave one."

"Your poor mother," Mrs. Rhibek added.

Toby undid his apron and draped it over the empty chair as though it were a guest at their table. He turned his order book face down next to the ketchup carousel and, without a word, headed for the door.

"Tobe?" the manager called after him, but Toby kept going.

It felt exhilarating to walk out, even if he knew he'd probably be back waiting tables the next day. It wasn't like he didn't need a job. Dave would take him back, and Toby would go, but for now, he felt victorious. Phil and Marcie Rhibek, what jackasses. *They never found a note?* Who? He and his mother? The police? If he and his mother found a note, why would he tell someone like Marcie Rhibek?

Later, there were phone messages from the manager and one or two friends on the waitstaff, but Toby didn't answer. How had he worked there so long? He should have walked out the first summer when he was fifteen and a dishwasher. The smell of the drain, no matter what people ate, nauseated him. Leftover food in the heat of summer had its own unchanging aroma above a sink full of steam. By the end of the evening, that smell permeated his nostrils, his clothing, his hair. He couldn't wait to go for a swim and a shower.

The next year he was promoted to busboy and Toby found satisfaction in matching people to the food left on their plates. Women on dates with whole entrées left uneaten, older ladies who'd leave just a few bites as if to signal something; the tubby guys who'd down three beers and clean everyone's plates plus the second basket of bread.

Now, as a waiter, Toby witnessed the torments people endured ordering food—the difficult scrutiny of the menu, indecision, second-guessing, regrets. Life itself! His father would have loved the stories Toby amused his mom with some mornings after work, when he acted out the parts.

That night, Toby told his mom he needed the car for a few hours, and to his surprise she didn't ask why. Once behind the wheel of her Taurus, he headed for New Vernon, the fishing town next door. TJ's was a waterfront hole where a kid he knew from high school tended bar. Everyone knew the place had no qualms about forgetting to check I.D.s.

"How's life among the fishes?" Jeff asked when he brought Toby his draft. Shaggy blond hair covered one eye. Like Toby, Jeff hadn't gone away to college with the rest of their class the year before. By day, he was a surfer.

"The Hut?" Toby took his first sip; he felt better. "I walked out today."

"You walked out?"

"Yeah, pretty stupid." Toby shrugged. "But I bet they'll take me back."

"Do you want to go back?" a voice asked from across the bar.

"Do I want to keep serving fried fish to tourists in Belle Harbor? Not really."

"I'm hiring." A muscular, bearded man in a baseball cap addressed Toby from a stool across the horseshoe-shaped bar. A neon beer sign blinked on and off above him.

"Hiring for what?"

"Fishing boat. The *Stella Marie*."

"I don't know anything about fishing." Toby took another swig of his beer. "I just dish 'em when they're cooked."

The guy laughed. "In that case, maybe we could use you in the galley."

"No, seriously," Toby said. "I don't think I'd do much on a fishing boat."

"Dude, it's not rocket science. Hauling nets, separating fish, icing them in the hold. You look pretty able. We're headed out in the morning, back in two weeks. I'm short one guy."

Toby had been pressing weights for years. He felt a twinge of accomplishment to be judged strong enough to do a job like that. Sometimes he still thought of himself as the same scrawny fifteen-year-old who started work at the Fish Hut.

He turned it over in his mind. "I dunno."

"Pay's good. You'd clear a couple thou. Maybe more, depending on the catch."

"Two K?" Toby repeated. "For two weeks?" The amount was more than he'd ever earned at the restaurant. His biggest week was eight hundred and that was during Schooner Fest.

"Think about it. I'm serious. Seven a.m. State Pier." The man extended his hand and Toby shook it. "Joe Moreno."

"Toby Osborne."

The bartender leaned across the counter once the captain had gone. "You're not thinking of doing that shit, are you?"

The neon logo continued to blink above the spot where the fisherman had been sitting; a rack of billiards clattered free in the adjacent room; another love song started on the jukebox. Toby saw his own face in the mirror. What did he have to lose? "I might," he said.

On the way home he called Megan. They'd been seeing each other over a year, though not very often. They lived in separate states. That week, she was vacationing with her family in the Berkshires. Toby remembered only a few times that his family went away on vacation. "You don't need a vacation when you live in a place as beautiful as Belle Harbor," his father used to tell him.

Megan's family owned what they called a cabin in the mountains, though the photos looked nicer than some rental cottages in town. Megan's father was a regional salesman for office supplies; her mom, a physical therapist, which Megan was studying to be too. When she graduated from high school, her parents gifted her a car. Toby received a thousand-dollar savings bond from his grandparents which, his mother explained, couldn't even be cashed for twenty years or something.

"Wait, what?" Megan cried when Toby told her what he'd done. They had a bad connection. "Hold on. Say it again. What did you do?"

"I know, right?"

"Toby, come on. Back up. What do you know about fishing?"

"Nothing. Not a thing. It's a joke anyone would even hire me."

"Are you serious? How is this a joke to you?"

"It's not. It's just. I don't know. A way out."

"Out of what?"

"The restaurant. The rut I've dug myself since my dad died."

He was aware of her silence on the other end. Toby hated talking over the phone. But that's what their long-distance relationship had become. Seeing each other five times a year. Talking on the phone.

"I get that," she said after a while. "Sort of."

He laughed. "I'll take that as a yes."

"But Toby—you'll be careful, okay?"

"Sure, yeah. It's a fishing trip. It's not like I'm heading off to war."

"You don't know what it's like."

"Come on."

"I'm sorry. You're right. I'm sure it will be fine," Megan said.

"No, you're right." He laughed. "I'm sure it won't."

"That's my Toby!" He heard her sigh. "Call me, okay? If you can."

"I'll try."

"I'm glad you quit the restaurant," she confessed when they said goodbye. "You deserve something better."

His mother was less enthused. "Toby, are you crazy? Two weeks on a fishing boat?"

"Two weeks is not long."

"Fourteen days can be a very long time."

"It would be good to get away. That's what I've been thinking. The last year—"

"I know it's been—"

"Hell."

"I know," his mom said. "But Toby—"

"What's the worst that could happen?"

"I can think of a few things."

In the end, she agreed. Technically she couldn't stop him. He was over eighteen.

"You made it," the captain shouted when he spotted Toby on the dock. He didn't look surprised, as though Moreno knew he'd show up. The boat backed away from its berth, accompanied by the smell of diesel smoke. Toby felt his stomach lurch;

he tasted the McDonald's breakfast sandwich he'd just gulped down at the back of his throat. He wondered what he'd done.

Just before heading out to sea, the *Stella Marie* made a final stop at the ice plant at the edge of the harbor. The boat bobbed beside the dock as a long hose shot a cascade of ice into the hold. Then they were steaming out of the harbor, passing anchored sailboats, returning fishing boats, the lighthouse. Multicolored houses climbed a hill above the steeple, all of it growing smaller, receding from view. The tang of sea air whipped past Toby's face.

An hour beyond the breakwater, they overtook a whale watch in the distance. Fragments of the tour guide's amplified voice echoed across the water. *We call this calf Suzie Q, and we've been tracking her in these waters every summer since—*

Moreno called Toby out of the hold to see a mother and her calf arc above the waves, splashing the pilothouse windows with spray. "Extra bonus, kid!" Moreno grinned. "You get to see whales. Tourists pay a hundred a pop for that."

His bunkmate was Tony Farini, a wiry handsome man about ten years older than Toby. Farini found significance in their names. "Tony! Toby! What do you know?" He invented a secret handshake between them on the spot. "So, I'm Anthony. Obviously. Toby is—?"

"Tobin."

"Tobin! That don't sound Italian," Farini joked. "What, are you rich?"

"No. We're not rich." Toby hadn't thought of his name that way before, but Farini was right. Tobin Osborne did sound rich. "I don't know where my parents got it from," he said.

"So, you're not like Tobin the Second?"

"No, man."

"That's good." Farini leaned back against the bunk wall, his face in shadow. "What's your old man called?"

"Tom. He's dead. He died last summer."

"That sucks."

"Totally."

"My old man's a prick," Farini said.

At dinner, an Aerosmith CD wailed on a boom box in the galley as the crew downed a microwaved meal of chicken nuggets and fries. Farini offered Toby a beer, but he turned it down. He never turned down a beer, but his stomach had begun to roll with the swells. When he stood to find his bunk, the floor rose with him. He had to brace himself against the wall to lurch his way down the dark corridor.

The next day, they set the net out to tow for a few hours until the captain blew the horn, and then it was time to haul back. Toby got into his oilskins and boots and joined the rest of the crew on deck. With the engine in neutral, the boat drifted without sound until the winch was put in gear and the process of hauling back the net began.

Once the net was out of the water, Farini latched it to the aft deck door. An older crewman named Muldoon fixed it to the stanchion at the stern. Toby stood shoulder to shoulder with two men balancing on the slick deck as, hand over hand, they hauled the net up, piece by piece, flailing with fish.

The cord end was the most important, Farini told him, because that's where you opened the net at the bottom for the fish to come pouring onto the deck. Haddock, cod, halibut, flounder, monkfish, whatever was in the net needed to be culled and separated. The head of the monkfish had to be cut off and the tails, which Farini told him tasted like scallops, had to be separated. That was the job the captain gave Toby. When all this was done, the entire catch had to be iced down in the hold. Farini was the hold man. His job was to chop the ice with a metal tool and shovel it onto the fish as they were loaded into the hold.

Then they did the same thing over again the next day.

Toby stayed to himself, did what was asked. He earned a grudging respect from Moreno and the crew for the meals he cooked out of whatever he found on board: fish chowder; cheese, potato and bacon omelets. His father had taught him how to cook. Toby remembered him in his maroon bathrobe and flannel pajamas making pancakes and eggs on Sundays. Farini, who had crewed on more boats than any of them, offered faint praise. "Anything's better than chicken nuggets."

Toby collapsed into his bunk each night, exhausted. With time on his hands, alone, he wondered about Megan, what she'd be doing that minute. Other nights, random memories returned. One year, for his birthday, his parents gave him a hamster, when what he wanted was a dog. His father was allergic. It drove Toby crazy to see the thing scrambling around its cage on his dresser, wildly running nowhere on a plastic wheel.

At school that fall, he traded the hamster and its cage for a stack of baseball cards.

Megan would still be at her family's cabin in the mountains. That afternoon, she'd have gone with her friends to the lake. He pictured her playing board games with her younger sister in the kitchen, eating ice cream on the porch. Toby had to borrow the car from his mother whenever he visited her in college. He wondered if maybe they should split up before she went back to Vermont that fall. Both of them could move on, find someone new. Other nights, he thought that his heart would break if they did. Maybe in the end, they'd even wind up getting married. He wasn't sure which outcome he wanted.

One night, Farini brought two beers back to their bunk and this time Toby took one. He tried to think what they had in common to start a conversation. "Was your father a fisherman, too?" he finally offered.

"My old man? Nah. He owns a bar. My old man's a drunk."

One question and he was off.

"My mom's an addict. She was back then. I was born addicted, ain't that a way to start out life? A newborn addicted to pills. My old man pushed my ma down a flight of stairs, and she wound up on Vicodin. Vicodin, Percocet, whatever she could get her hands on. Back then the drug companies said no way it's habit-forming. Guess what?"

Farini drummed a rhythm on his knee, bouncing up and down to the beat. "Then I got hit by a car when I was ten. Wound up on painkillers, too. My old man used to come up to say goodnight and he'd pop up one of my bedside meds like it was candy. I thought that was chill for a while, but it stopped being funny when the bottles started turning up empty.

"Long story short, I come from an epic line of addicts. Whatever's on hand, I'll take it. Alcohol, pot, heroin for a while. Kicked heroin," Farini said.

He was silent, and Toby wondered if he was through. Toby's life in Belle Harbor, five miles from New Vernon, seemed like a fairytale planet.

"Yeah, got off smack, but not before I had a kid with a girl who won't let me see him no more." Farini popped a second beer. "Not that I blame her. Toby, dude, I don't blame anyone."

He took a long gulp of beer. Farini stopped drumming on his legs. His hands tapped a few more beats on the beer can. "I've got an older kid, too. Pretty much the same story with his mom, the ex-wife. Won't let me see him. What would I be if not for dope, man. Maybe a house, a nice porch, the yard, blahdablah-blahblah. I'm basically homeless now. Either I'm crewing or I'm crashing somewhere 'til they toss me out. Then I get a room above the bar on Jones Street. That place is evil, man. Stay out of there."

"Are you still—" Toby searched for the word.

"Using? No, quit that shit. I did. Still on OxyContin, though. Just to keep the even keel. Maintenance, Tobe. Take your edge off. Done with smack, though. It's all under control. 'I'm the master of my own fate,' right man? What's that poem you learn in school? You said your mom writes poetry, right?"

Toby nodded, his mind revving, unable to stitch together a few words of encouragement. It all sounded lame. "Do you ever think about quitting?"

"Quitting? Yeah. Every day. When the time is right, bro. Can't do that now. When the time is right."

"That'll be good," Toby offered feebly. He felt like a fool.

He was lying in his lower bunk after dinner a few nights later. He was looking at his phone, the paperback he'd been reading open on his lap. Farini entered without a word. Toby watched him open his duffel, remove a white shirt and tie, followed by a suit of the same color. He hung them from the top bunk, the jacket on its hanger swaying above Toby's head.

"What are you, John Travolta?" Toby laughed. "What's up with the white suit?"

"It's the suit I was married in, man. My lucky suit."

"Are you feeling lucky?" Toby asked.

"You tell me."

Farini got out of his work clothes and slipped on the suit pants, the white shirt. He knotted the tie and slid his arms into the jacket, all without a word.

"A white suit!" Toby kept at him. "Why would you bring a suit on a fishing boat?"

"It's a suit," Farini said.

"Yeah, I know but—it's not like you're going anywhere."

"Fuck off."

"Okay." Toby watched Farini hunch through the door. "You too."

Toby liked to walk the upper deck before sleep, contemplating the stars, thinking about his father. Where was he now?

His father used to love looking at the stars. The light from the pilothouse seemed comforting. Sounds drifted up from below, music, laughter, the big nets rocking in the wind, the deck slick beneath his feet, the smell of fish.

Toby had just picked out Cassiopeia in the northern sky when Tony Farini suddenly appeared in the corner of his eye. Before Toby knew what was happening, Farini had clambered onto the railing, one hand loosely circling the stanchion, the other floating free over the water like a benediction. He leaned out over the edge.

Toby rushed toward him. "Hey! What are you doing, man? Hold up!"

Farini looked down at him. "It's all bullshit, right?"

"No. It's not."

Toby, who'd long believed this to be true, managed to summon another view. It wasn't bullshit. Life wasn't bullshit. It was a gift, precious and fleeting.

Farini graced him with a distant smile. "And so says you." He turned back to the water. His suit jacket flapped open in the breeze.

"Wait!" Toby yelled, but Farini was already gone, leaping from the railing into the foaming dark below, his body an apparition of white flashing by.

Toby glanced over his shoulder for a life preserver, but the one lashed below the pilothouse would take too long to untie. Without thinking, he whipped off his boots and his belt and vaulted over the rail to plunge into the rolling ocean. For a moment, he was twelve again, leaping off Jake's boat to swim to shore. But this wasn't the short summer dive off a cabin cruiser—this jump was scarier, much higher up. The shock of hitting the waves stopped his heart. The sea was high. It was night and he couldn't see where Farini had landed. August, but the water was cold.

A spotlight turned on above the pilothouse; the horn blasted, and Muldoon ran up on deck from below. The captain swept the surf with the spotlight and Toby spotted Farini. He looked angry but desperate, too, thrashing against the waves. Fighting the swells, Toby managed to swim to where he struggled in the water. He grabbed him in a chokehold and punched Farini hard in the temple. He slumped into Toby's arms, and someone above tossed down a line.

Toby clutched the unconscious man as they were hauled back on board, his hand circling the other man's waist. It took a moment for Toby to realize what the object inside Farini's suit pocket was. A syringe.

"Hero Fisherman" was the front-page headline in the weekly paper when they docked days later. All that week, wherever he went, Toby saw those words blaring above his photo from every *Village News* vending machine in town. He couldn't figure out where they'd gotten the story until Muldoon admitted it was his sister.

In local word of mouth, it all became muddled. Tony Farini hadn't jumped overboard intentionally but was swept off the deck by a rogue wave. And Toby Osborne was a hero.

They asked him to be Marshall of the fall parade, to ride in the head convertible with the Harvest Queen, but Toby said no.

"Are you sure?" his mom asked.

"Mom, come on," he answered.

"No, I know." She laughed. "I can't see you doing it either. All that attention."

"I'm not a hero," Toby said.

"I don't know. Not many people would have done what you did."

"Sure they would."

"You're lucky you're such a strong swimmer."

"I didn't stop to think about it. I just jumped in."

"Weren't you scared?" she asked, as people always would, even years later.

Toby didn't remember being scared. Watching Farini balanced on the rail, poised between worlds, Toby glimpsed his father.

CHAPTER 17

Return

TOBY AND HIS MOTHER watched from the safety of an upstairs window as a limb of the old willow crashed into the cottage next door, scattering shingles into the wind. The power had been out since the night before, snow as deep as either of them had ever seen, their old house creaking in the wind. It sounded as though an angry bear was thumping through the attic.

They were still riveted to the window a few minutes later when the mighty willow swayed for a few beats as though waltzing in the wind, then toppled over in slow motion, landing in a snowbank like a fairytale giant. The wind shrieked overhead; the impact shook their house. The willow's upended roots were nearly as tall as the cottage.

Toby retrieved his phone from his back pocket and snapped a photo.

Catharine took a step back from the window. "I can't believe we just saw that."

She remembered the tree when it was healthy and strong, the weeping green branches extending to the lawn, shifting in the breeze. It reminded her of the beautiful Public Garden willows she and Tom used to sit beneath that summer they met, a dreamlike memory of being in love, feeling caressed by the willow's graceful arms.

A long time, too, since the willow next door resembled the monumental ones in Boston. Over the years, Catharine watched it shrink, limbs lopped off one by one, the remaining branches twisted and bare. The tree should have been taken down years ago, as close as it stood to the cottage. If the owners in Florida ever made it north, they would have known that. But the owners never did.

Catharine felt sorry for the tree. She felt sorry for the little house battered by snow and winds, trying to withstand nature's assault. She and Toby were still gazing at the fallen giant below when another gust picked up a broken branch and hurled it like a spear through one of the cottage's front windows, the sound of shattering glass mingling with the wind.

"Oh man," Toby said. "I feel like I should go over there and board that place up before the snow gets in."

"Don't you go out there!" Catharine ordered as though her adult son were still a boy within her command. "You could get hurt," she added in a softer tone.

"Mom."

"You could."

He'd been living at home for a few months by then. He'd come back to Belle Harbor to regroup after moving out of the place he shared with Megan in Boston. That summer she'd graduated from B.U. and found a physical therapy job at Mass General. By Christmas, she'd met a doctor. He wasn't surprised.

Toby had spent the first few weeks home trying not to think about his life. One day his old high school shop teacher recommended him for a carpentry job, and he discovered he liked renovating old houses. The smell of wood, designing things. At night, he tinkered with inventions in his mother's basement, just as he had when he was twelve. Sometimes he pictured his father in his bathrobe on the staircase, poking his head downstairs the way he used to, checking on what Toby was up to. *How's it going down there, Steve Jobs?*

Toby was having breakfast at a coffee shop in town the morning a few weeks later when he heard the news about the cottage. The children in Florida who'd inherited the property years ago had decided to sell rather than pay what it would cost to salvage it. Even in Florida, viewing the damage in photos, the extent of what was needed would have been obvious. Toby made a lowball offer before it ever went on the market. He and his mother composed a letter to the owners. They were giddy writing it. How much the place had meant to them over the years. The enjoyment they derived from watching vacationing renters.

"Did we really just say that?" Catharine laughed.

"In a sense it's true," Toby reminded her. "You did occasionally enjoy the show."

Toby wasn't sure what he'd do with the place once he renovated it, but it seemed an opportunity he shouldn't pass up. He'd had a little money since his grandfather died; he had the skills, he'd find the time to work on it in his spare time. He already decided that if he sold the place, it would have to be to someone who'd live there. He'd stipulate that in the sales contract. No more weekly renters to harass his long-suffering mom.

Or maybe she might live there? His mother could sell the big old house and downsize to the cottage. He'd float that idea once the work was finished. Toby took extra care with the details he thought she might like. The finish carpentry on the built-in bookshelves, the carved mantel above the fireplace. He could see her there with a book beside the fire. He pictured her with a cat.

He was on a ladder behind the cottage one afternoon late that summer, prying off shingles with a crowbar, when he heard a car door slam. Toby swiveled his head to see who it was, but the hedge blocked his view. The boxwood had grown taller over the years. Toby's own house across the way seemed more distant from its neighbor than it had when he was a boy, the sound of raucous summer renters punctuating his sleep.

He climbed down from the ladder and circled around to the front yard where a young woman stood beside an old Mercedes. Toby knew who she was the minute he saw her copper-penny hair in the sun. He remembered the silver car, too. It had looked new the last time he saw it.

"I'm sorry." The woman took a step backward toward the car. Toby saw a patch of rust on the driver's door. "I didn't know anyone would be here. I didn't see a car."

"That's okay." Toby waved away her apology. "Are you looking for someone?"

"Not really." The stranger shook her head. "I just wanted to have a peek for a minute, if that's okay."

"Sure. Walk around if you want. No one lives here."

Toby studied her profile. The expression on her face wasn't nostalgia. "I stayed here once years ago, my family and I."

"I thought so," Toby said, wondering if he should have.

Toby and his father had watched from the upstairs window while the girl was handcuffed and loaded into a police car. How scary that had seemed then. She'd come back, the ghost who haunted his memory. The summer his mother was in Ireland, the last summer that things were ever okay, before his father grew steadily worse. And then he died.

The girl looked confused. "Why would you know that? That I've been here before."

"I grew up next door." Toby gestured behind him. "I recognize you. Your hair."

The girl touched a hand to her skull. "Right. Hard not to recognize." Her laugh carried in the wind.

"That's the same car your family had back then, right?"

"Yep. Hand-me-down from dad." She flashed him a sideways grin. "Not looking so hot now." She tilted her head and eyed him quizzically. "But how do you remember our car?"

Toby looked down at his feet then met her eye once more. "I wasn't like stalking you or anything, but my bedroom window's right up there. I couldn't help noticing you." He didn't want to tell her that he'd also seen her arrested. "I have a memory of you standing with one hand on your hip, yellow shorts. Your father was giving you a hard time about something."

"That sounds right." She laughed.

"I heard you say, 'Really?' Like—*really?* I wanted to sound like that."

"How old were you?"

"I don't know. Fifteen?"

"I think I maybe saw you, too. I was the same age." She hesitated. "You seemed pretty young then."

"I probably was." He smiled. "I'm Tobin, by the way." Toby had started using his full name after he moved back to Belle Harbor. "Toby" was a kid's name, and he was no longer a kid. Most people still called him Toby, though, even his mom. She'd make a conscious effort to call him "Tobin," but then she'd catch herself and say, "I'm sorry, I just never pictured having to call you that."

"I'm Bree." The girl reached out her hand and smiled.

"I don't know why I used 'Tobin' just then. Everyone calls me Toby."

"So listen, Tobin-Toby, do you want a beer?"

Toby tried to cover his surprise. What was she doing driving around with beer in her car after what happened? He thought about it for a second. "Sure," he agreed.

Bree opened the driver's door. Toby unbuckled his toolbelt and left it on the ground. He opened the passenger door to take a seat beside her. He wondered if his mother could see him if she happened to look out an upstairs window. What did it matter if she did? Still, he got in quickly and shut the door. Bree reached into a cooler in the back seat and handed him a cold bottle. She twisted off her cap and took a long swallow. "I'm a bad influence."

Toby thought for a moment, wondering if he should say this but then he did. "Do you always blame yourself?"

"What?" She laughed.

"You know."

"I don't."

"Not everything has to be your fault."

Bree gazed out the driver's window. She tilted back her head and took another sip of beer. "I remember your father sitting under that tree there. I was doing yoga stretches in my short shorts, flashing my bum in his face. I wanted him to look. I wanted him to want me. I willed him to look up and see me."

"Did he?"

"No. He was reading a book. He didn't even notice."

"That sounds like him." Toby smiled at this vision of his dad. Lolita flirting with him from across the lawn, Tom Osborne unaware, reading a book. "My dad died a few summers later," Toby said. "The year I graduated from high school."

"Oh gosh, I'm sorry."

"No, it's fine. I mean, not fine, but it's a long time ago now."

"I think about him sometimes. Reading on your lawn, under that tree. That was the afternoon before it happened. That's why it's etched in my brain. That was the same day I hit that girl in the woods."

"Gabriela."

"Gabriela Ortiz," Bree added.

"She didn't die, you know."

"I know."

"She came back to school."

"But she has brain damage, right?"

"Not really," Toby said. "I don't think so anyway. She's in a wheelchair."

"I live with that every day."

"She has two kids now. I saw them in town together last week. Her husband runs a landscaping business. I think she's doing okay." The girl put her hands on the steering wheel. She lowered her head.

Toby said, "You should know that."

"You don't have to try and make me feel better."

"It's true."

Bree nodded. "I know what people said about me. The rich girl from Connecticut who got off easy. I read the online chats."

Toby looked down. "Something like that."

"We weren't rich, just so you know. Especially afterwards. I cried myself to sleep every night for years. I still do whenever I let myself think about what happened. I've never gotten over that day. My father calls it my 'failure to launch.' That's great, isn't it? 'Failure to launch.' Like I'm a rocket ship. I guess maybe you already figured that out from the rusted-out hand-me-down car."

Toby wondered if the same phrase didn't apply to him. *Failure to launch.* He reached out to place a hand on her shoulder. "I'm sorry," he said. She folded into his arms, sobbing against his chest. He didn't know what to do. He rested his head on the top of hers, as though comforting a child. She raised her face to his and their lips met.

"I shouldn't have done that," Toby said.

"You didn't."

Up close, the emptiness in her eyes warned him away.

"I told you I was a bad influence," she said.

Toby took a deep breath. "Look—," he began.

"No, I know." She cut him off. "I'm really sorry."

"You don't have to be sorry. Not to me. It's just—I'm just coming out of a relationship and things are—"

"Complicated?" She held up a hand. "Stop," she said. "Please."

Toby realized that perhaps he hadn't admitted as much in words before, how broken he'd been since he and Megan split up. She wanted someone else. He couldn't blame her. Sometimes Toby feared that maybe it was inside him, a void, the reason he couldn't sustain a relationship. Maybe his father had it, too.

They sat together in silence for a time. She took a sip of beer. "So what do you do? Are you a contractor?"

"I guess I am. Not what I figured I'd be doing, but hey."

"What did you figure you'd be doing?"

Toby thought for a moment. "I don't know. Working in an office probably. Sitting at a computer. I guess I didn't have big dreams."

"Me neither."

It surprised him to have said this. There was a time he wanted to do things, to be an architect, an engineer, but it turned out he hated math. "What I just said, that's not totally true," Toby corrected himself. "I always did want to build things."

"Now you have." Bree raised her bottle as a toast and Toby obliged, leaning over to clink hers.

"Getting there," he said.

After a while she spoke again. "Those boys that night, the boys she was running away from. Gabriela. Do you know what happened to them?"

Toby hadn't thought about either of those guys in years. In high school, they were the hoodlum twins, Rick and Rob, though they weren't related. It was a small town, so Toby did know what had become of them. "Rick's in Concord—the prison—for pushing fentanyl, I think. Rob joined the Army. Did a couple tours in Afghanistan. He's out now."

Bree exhaled. "I never thought I'd come back here. You know what I used to call this place? 'Nowhere Town.' My parents vacationed in Belle Harbor every summer. After that last time, we never came back again." She put her hands on the wheel. "Seeing it again, thinking about that day, I was such an empty idiot back then."

"Everyone's an idiot growing up," Toby said.

"I'm still a mess." Bree shook her head. "That's my punishment. I'm not in a wheelchair. I don't look like I'm damaged. I'm just someone who can't figure out why it's worth doing anything."

Bree took a long sip of beer and sighed. "Anyway. I should go. It's getting late."

"You're okay?"

"I've only had one beer!"

"I mean—in general. Tomorrow. Next year. Are you going to be okay?"

"Who knows?"

Toby put his hand on the passenger door. He turned to face her. "You may not believe this, but I thought about you a lot over the years."

"You thought about me?"

"You seemed so sad that night. Sad and small and afraid when my dad and I watched you get pushed into the back of that police car."

Bree wiped her eyes. "Great, now I'm crying again."

"I didn't mean for you to cry."

She put a hand on his. "It's okay," she said. "I like a good cry."

Toby waited for her to wipe her eyes. She looked out the driver's window. "I like your house, by the way."

"You like our house?"

"It's got character."

"Thanks. That's what my mom says." Toby opened the car door. "Listen, I hope one day it all—"

"Maybe it will." Bree smiled. She put the car in reverse and Toby got out.

He rapped once on the passenger window as she pulled away. "Take care of yourself."

"Keep on building," Bree said, waving as she pulled away.

It was late afternoon. He was done for the day. Toby put away his tools. He didn't want to go back to his house just then, to have a conversation with his mom. He took a walk down the street to the cove where his father died.

Toby sat on the ledge where the cops found his bathrobe and slippers. The water was flat as glass, blue ribbons out to the horizon. He thought how life can turn on an instant. Bree, Gabriela, his dad. What was going through his father's mind that day? Anything? Nothing? What were his thoughts as he folded his bathrobe and stepped over the rocks into the frigid ocean?

He wondered when he'd get over Megan. They'd split up and gotten back together so many times, he should be over her by now and yet he wasn't. He'd seen other women over the years whenever they were taking a break. Monthlong summer romances when he stayed with his mom in Belle Harbor. He wondered how those women thought of him now back in their city apartments and reunited with the boyfriends they thought they were breaking up with, how they remembered their fling with the handyman in Belle Harbor.

His mother was taking a chicken out of the oven when he came through the back door.

"I'm taking the car, okay?"

He saw that she wanted to ask where he was going, but they'd forged a delicate balance whenever Toby returned to live at home for a while. "Not hungry?" was all she asked.

"I'll eat later." He took the keys off the hook and kissed her forehead, then drove one town over to New Vernon.

TJ's never changed. When he walked in, it could have been the night he signed up for the *Stella Marie*. The same neon sign blinked above the horseshoe bar, the periodic sound of billiards crackled in the next room, the smell of sawdust and beer. His surfer friend Jeff still worked there tending bar, years after high school. He was probably the happiest person Toby knew. Toby felt himself forever spinning wheels, waiting for the next step in life to somehow reveal itself. He wondered if that was how his father had felt, teaching year after year at the community college in the city, the job that was supposed to have been a temporary stop, not his whole career.

"Did you hear about your buddy?" Jeff asked as he set down Toby's beer.

"Who?"

"The guy you saved."

"Tony Farini," Toby said.

"He OD'd the other day."

"What?"

"He was just in here last week," Jeff said. "Definitely on something, dude."

"Wait," Toby said. "He OD'd, like he died?"

"Yeah. Pretty fucked up."

Toby left his beer on the counter and went to stand outside. He inhaled the sea air, the chill of a September night, fishing boats tied up at the pier bobbing with the tide, moorings sounding their rhythm in the wind. He took a deep breath and let a howl escape into the air. In New Vernon, nobody cared. He allowed himself to cry.

The funeral was at Our Lady of the Sea, what everyone called the Italian church, to distinguish it from the smaller stone Catholic chapel, the tourist church. To the left of Toby's pew, the statue of a silver-robed Madonna extended her hands in pity; the sorrow in her eyes seemed genuine.

Toby felt like an old man in the suit he'd bought that summer for a friend's wedding. The younger men were mostly in jeans and T-shirts, the women in short skirts and lacy party dresses. Older women were dressed all in black, kerchiefs around their heads. He thought again of Farini's white suit, the one he wore to his wedding.

"Let us pray," the priest pronounced at the steps of the altar just before the coffin was rolled down the aisle to the waiting hearse. "We who are left behind mourn the loss of a son, a brother, a father, but Anthony himself now rejoices as he returns to his one true home."

Toby hoped it would be better than the one he grew up in.

"May the Lord welcome him. In the name of the Father, and of the Son—"

In the front pew, Farini's mother let out a sob. Beside her, a young woman shifted her long black curls and leaned against the older woman's shoulder. Farini's father sat by himself in a pew across the aisle. A young boy sat behind him.

Toby tried to remember what the Unitarian minister had said at his father's service, but he had no memory of the words. The priest was descending from the altar to sprinkle holy water on the flag-draped casket. Toby was surprised to realize Farini was a veteran, though when he thought about it, there wasn't much he actually knew about the man whose life he'd saved.

The organist struck a chord, and the congregation joined in "For Those in Peril on the Sea" as the casket rolled down the aisle, accompanied by six men who looked like football players. Farini's family formed a receiving line in the vestibule. Toby watched Tony's mother lean forward to kiss a friend. The girl with the black curls stood between Farini's divorced parents. She must have been his sister.

When Toby introduced himself, Tony's father greeted him with a pained smile. "If it isn't the Hero. Guess old Tony could've used another rescue the other night, hey bud?"

Toby smelled the alcohol on his breath. He heard Farini's voice echo in his head. *My father's a prick.*

Farini's sister rolled her eyes. "Dad."

"What? Am I wrong? What do you think, Hero?"

"I'm sorry for your loss," Toby said as he moved away. Now he sounded like an old man, too.

At the end of the line, a little removed from the rest of the family, stood the young boy he'd seen seated toward the front. Toby recognized him then. Tony Farini's son, the ten-year-old boy his ex-wife wouldn't let him see. His son looked just like him. The dark, almost black eyes, his strong profile.

"Toby Osborne." He put a hand on the boy's shoulder. "You must be his son."

"Mario."

"I like your name."

The boy laughed at that. "You were like his best friend, right?"

Toby hoped his face didn't register his surprise. "I don't know, man."

The son's expectant look told him he should say more. "He was a great guy," Toby said.

"You saved his life."

"I wish I could have."

Toby was aware of a woman watching their conversation from just outside the vestibule. Toby recognized her from the wallet photo Farini had shown him. The ex-wife, Mario's mother.

She stood chain-smoking cigarettes just outside the doors, glancing back to check on who her boy was speaking to in the receiving line. Mario's mother was with another man. Toby tried to recall what Farini had told him about her, but the only vivid detail he called up was the white suit. Farini's syringe in the pocket, when they were finally hauled back on board.

Toby dug out one of his business cards from his wallet and slipped it into the boy's palm. "Give me a call. If you want. If you need anything."

"I will," the boy said. "Thanks."

He stepped outside into the sunlight which seemed too bright after the interior of the church. Small clusters of mourners gathered on the lawn. Toby saw that Farini's casket was already loaded into the hearse. A colorful TV van beneath a satellite dish idled by the curb. Another OD death in Massachusetts. Was that still news?

A young woman with a notepad strode toward him as he made his way to the sidewalk.

"Excuse me?" she called.

The sun glinted off her glasses; she confronted him with intelligent dark eyes. The way she held her pen against her note-book evoked his mom and her dedication all those decades to whatever she was writing. The few times she'd showed him a poem, Toby had no idea what she was talking about.

"*Boston Globe*." She flashed a press pass from her pocket.

Toby wondered why she'd picked him out. Maybe because he was one of the few mourners heading back to their cars alone.

"Were you a friend of his?" the reporter asked.

Toby paused. "No, not a friend." Farini's son's words returned to him. "I guess I saved his life once."

"You're Toby Osborne?"

"Tobin," he corrected, then laughed. "Toby. Right, Toby Osborne." He extended a hand.

She shook his and said, "I was hoping I'd find you."

"Find me how?"

"Okay, well—" She looked a little chagrined. "I took a peek at the archives, the *Stella Marie*. I saw your photo. I thought that was you."

"I don't understand. Why is this a story for the *Boston Globe*? Or the evening news? Isn't there an opioid death every day now?"

"I guess because of you."

"What?"

"Because he didn't die those years ago. Because you saved his life and now—It brings it home somehow. The real life behind the headline. It's pretty sad."

"Yeah, it is," Toby agreed and for the first time that morning he felt something, he felt the weight of Tony Farini's lost life.

He glanced at the hearse idling at the curb, blinkers on. People were heading for their cars. "He had a rough life," Toby said. "I'd hoped maybe a second chance might—you know." The reporter gazed at him expectantly. Toby realized he should finish the sentence. She was waiting for a quote. "I hoped maybe a second chance would be what he needed, to turn his life around. Like in the movies."

"Or in books?" The reporter jotted a line and looked up again.

"My mother's a writer actually. I should have said 'books.'"

"What does she write?"

"Poetry. Catharine Osborne."

"She's your mother?" The reporter laughed. "I love your mom's poetry."

Toby shook his head. "Seriously? How do you know my mother's poetry?"

"I have her book," the reporter said. "I bought it years ago at a used bookstore in Somerville. The inscription she wrote pulled me in. 'Happily Ever After!' It was dated like days before 9/11. I bought the book and I loved her poems. I always wondered how that other woman's life turned out. The one she was wishing a happy life. But that's me, the reporter looking for a story."

"I'm sorry, you are?"

"Jennifer Almon."

"Jennifer! Hi. Could I like—introduce you to my mom? You don't know how happy that would make her."

"Wow." She laughed and Toby caught another glimpse of her profile, the arc of her hands in the air, gesturing with her pen and notebook. "Meeting your mom. That was fast!"

The ease of her laughter made it seem as though he already knew her; had always known her. He'd been waiting for her to show up and now she had. In that moment, he saw their future. Where had it come from? He hadn't seen it coming. He didn't deserve it.

Yes, he did.

Happy ever after.

CHAPTER 18

The Heart at Rest

"It's probably nothing," Catharine told Toby on the phone, echoing the same words her doctor used a few days earlier. "They want me to come in for some tests."

"What tests?"

"A stress test and an echocardiogram."

"Mom."

"No, it's okay."

She hoped that was true. For weeks, she'd been feeling winded and lightheaded. Sometimes Catharine woke at night with the sense of her heart flipping in her chest.

"I'll come up. I'll take you to the hospital," Toby said. "When is it?"

"You don't have to."

"I've got a crew now, Mom. I can take a few days off."

Toby was renovating old houses in Somerville and Cambridge that summer. He and Jennifer lived in one of them. She was expecting their first child.

"Are you sure?"

"Mom," he said again, this time with a laugh.

The night before the procedure, she dreamed of Tom. He looked the way he had when Toby was little. He was dressed in his favorite blue shirt. "I didn't drown myself on purpose," is what he'd come to tell her. "Though I never blamed you for wondering."

"I knew you didn't," she answered. "Inside, I've always known that."

"My heart gave out." He ran his hands through his hair in that way he had. "But yours won't. You're going to be okay, Cat."

"How do you know that?" she asked.

"I know a lot of things now."

Catharine gazed at a pockmarked acoustic ceiling the next morning as her gurney slowly rolled inside a humming machine. Her heart had been shot through with radioactive dye, and now a big drum rotated from side to side across her chest. How strange to see this first glimpse of her own mortality.

At fifty-eight, she was years beyond the age her parents reached. They died young, a year apart, stubborn to the end. Their funerals took place in a rented hall, rather than St. Bart's or the temple. All their lives, neither would convert.

Catharine's mother was religious mostly in the kitchen, a devotion to her family's recipes beloved at the deli: Rachel's rugelach, her plum cake and noodle kugel. Though her father seldom went to mass once Catharine left for college, he never stopped carrying his rosary beads. Catharine didn't think she could put into words what she believed, except that there was a spiritual world greater than this one even if organized religions seldom grasped it. One life on earth was not the end. How could it be?

When she was younger, Catharine hoped to grow old like graceful Emma Nolan or her next-door neighbor, Maureen O'Malley. Neighbors still told stories of how she'd smoke Virginia Slims in a cigarette holder, a woman who brought her own cocktail shaker and martini glass to backyard barbecues.

Tom would have hated growing old.

At night, in those weeks after he died, Catharine had locked herself in his study, digging through his papers and notebooks, hoping for a clue. She flipped through his beloved Bob Slate notebooks, the ones he kept locked away in a metal toolbox. Catharine thumbed through a few; she learned nothing.

His newer writing was tucked inside a thick leather folder, dozens of heavily corrected typewritten pages, all facing in different directions, as though he were constantly reading through the file, turning over pages, losing his place, rereading, rearranging, putting those pages aside for months or years at a time. Which was so like Tom. She could see him returning to the same file over and over, never quite satisfied, unable to move on.

Catharine never found what she was looking for hunting through his papers, a hint of certainty, a reason why Tom was gone. For years afterwards, she debated what to do with his work. She didn't want their son to find those pages one day. She was sorry she'd read them herself. The incompleteness, the pain, the unfulfilled longing he carried through his life. In the end, she persuaded the poetry review Tom once edited at Harvard to archive them. She wasn't sure if he would have loved or hated the idea. She liked to imagine a researcher stumbling upon his papers one day. Maybe they would understand; he'd find the reader he'd been seeking.

The machine beeped three times and then it was over, the stretcher slowly retracing its path backwards, reversing the journey. Returned to life, Catharine noticed a 3-D image of a beating heart rotating slowly in place on a computer screen across the room. Two hearts. One turning from side to side like a show-off runway model; the second at rest.

"Is that me?" Catharine asked, and the technician nodded.

How surreal to see her own living heart aglow on a computer screen. Hello! Over here. *I'm your heart.* Surreal and also profound. Technology had surpassed her capacity for surprise, but here was her beating heart.

"Everything's good. No cause for alarm," the doctor told her on the phone a few days later. "Of course, we'll keep an eye on your numbers down the road."

She felt newly free, an entire summer vacation before her. Weeks that were her own. After she'd fulfilled one more obligation, that is. A visit to Tom's mother, the dreaded trip she made each summer. First, the long drive to the nursing home in Lexington, traffic worse every year, then the hour spent trying to make conversation with a woman who often no longer recognized her, and when she did, seldom seemed to appreciate the company.

Catharine spotted her mother-in-law from a distance, already waiting by a window near the garden. She wore a droopy straw hat, pearls and a pink suit, her stockings bagging at her shins, unlaced Reeboks on her feet. Catharine should talk to one of the aides before she left. Someone could at least tie her shoes. The old Polly would have been mortified.

"There you are!" Her face brightened when she spotted Catharine in the doorway. "I have news!"

Catharine took a seat beside her and grasped her mother-in-law's hands. Polly still wore the same chunky rings she always had, though now they spun loose on her fingers.

"What news?"

"I've changed my name!" she announced. "Do you want to know what it is?" Her sly sideways smile reminded Catharine of a child sharing a secret.

"Of course."

"Gladdie!"

"Oh." Catharine struggled to compose a neutral expression. "How did you decide on that?"

"Gladys is my middle name."

"That makes sense then." Catharine tried to think of something else to say. "So that's what everyone calls you now?"

Her mother-in-law looked deflated. "No."

"Ah."

Polly leaned forward and peered at Catharine with a sharp look. "And who are you?"

"I'm Catharine. Tom's wife."

"Poor Tom." The old woman sighed. "He's still dead, isn't he?"

It was not the first time Tom's mother had asked that question. The look on her face always made Catharine want to cry. "Yes," she said. "He has been for a while."

They sat together in silence. "I never understood how you didn't figure it out," Polly said at last, as though she'd been speaking all along.

"Figure what out?" Catharine asked.

"How damaged my Tom was when you married him."

Catharine indulged the fantasy of closing her hands around Polly's throat, squeezing that string of pearls around her neck, what it would feel like if only for an instant to strangle her mother-in-law. *How I never figured it out?* Why didn't you tell me? Instead, Tom's mother had invested Catharine on her wedding day with the duty of saving her brilliant boy.

Catharine crossed her hands in her lap. She took a deep breath. "How could you pretend all those years there was nothing wrong with Tom?"

Polly stared at her blankly. "There was nothing wrong with Tom."

"You just said there was."

"Is that what I said?"

And she was gone, withdrawn into her familiar daze, a half-smile playing on her lips, her eyes no longer focused on her visitor but on some private amusement. Catharine looked out at the little patio beside the rose garden.

Polly snapped awake once more. "Tom did love his father, you know," she said with urgency. "He might not have always shown it, but he loved his father."

"And your husband felt the same," Catharine added. The words came out as a question Polly didn't answer.

"Do you know what's the worst thing about this cruise ship?" she asked.

Catharine shook her head.

"They steal things. The cabin boy stole my slippers."

These visits always ended the same way, with Polly complaining. Catharine liked to think that if she ever wound up being cared for by strangers, she'd find something to be grateful for.

"Do you want me to speak to the captain?"

Polly sighed. "What good would it do?"

"Shall we look for your slippers in your room?"

"I'm sure they'll turn up."

"I bet they will," Catharine said.

"Are you the new nurse?" Polly asked.

"I'm Catharine, Tom's wife."

"That's right." Polly shut her eyes for a few moments. When she looked up, she seemed at peace. "All for the best, though, isn't it?" she said. "All for the best." Her gaze lighted on Catharine then drifted to the door. "Are you staying for lunch? Not that I'd recommend it. The food here is awful."

The text from Gavin Royce came as a surprise that August. They'd exchanged a few messages in the past, usually around Christmas those first few years after her trip to Dublin. There'd been no falling out, no particular reason to drift out of touch, yet Catharine knew the likelihood they'd ever see each other again was remote. One year, it struck her as she packed away Christmas ornaments that it had been two years since they'd exchanged holiday greetings, and then it was five, and now she'd lost touch with how long it had been. Recently it came to her that she was now the exact age he'd been when they met. He'd seemed so much older at the time.

"I'm still waiting," his message said.

"Gavin!" she texted back.

"Where is that book of poetry, Catharine Osborne?"

"One day, I'll send you one," she wrote back.

"You have a new book?"

"No," Catharine texted. "Not really. I'm thinking about publishing a few poems myself. I don't think that qualifies as a book."

"Of course it does!" Gavin replied. "Melville, Whitman, Virginia Woolf!"

Catharine stopped texting and phoned his number.

"Yes, I much prefer your voice," he answered. Catharine had always remembered the sound of his, the beautiful Scottish lilt to his words.

"So tell me, does hearing from you mean that you're finally coming to Boston?"

"Ah, that would be lovely," Gavin replied. "But no. The truth is I always imagined you'd visit here again one day. Everyone comes back to Dublin."

"I should have. It was my turn to buy you dinner."

"Alas," Gavin said. "I don't travel anymore."

"Not at all?"

"I have a bit of trouble getting around some days," he said.

"Oh."

"Dublin is fine. Flying now, the way it is—I can't. Back surgery a while ago didn't go well. All those years clambering over mountains, bending over rocks. I'm seventy-one, you know. I'm afraid I'm a bit of a hobbler."

"I'm imagining you're an elegant one." Catharine laughed. "I just turned fifty-eight."

"Still a mere urchin!"

"It's so good to hear your voice."

"You sound the same."

Whenever Catharine thought of Gavin Royce and the brief time they'd spent together, what she felt was gratitude that nothing more had happened. She couldn't bear the thought of having hurt Tom that way. And yet, those few days were among the happiest in her life. She told him this now.

"For me, too," he said after a while. "The surprise of it. Not having expected much more in life after Sinéad. And then to meet you."

Catharine didn't want to end the call, to wait a few more years before she heard from him again. "Maybe we could do this from time to time, talk on the phone?"

"I'd like that," he said.

"What's your address? I'll force myself to do it. I'll send you a book of poems. I keep intending to make another chapbook. I always say I will one day, but I never do. I will. You've given me the inspiration. And a deadline, which is what I need. By the end of summer, I promise."

"I'll hold you to it."

"I'll do it next week. There's a bookstore in Harvard Square. It's quite amazing, really. You upload a file from your computer, and you print a book."

"Americans," Gavin said with a laugh.

"It's called the Espresso Machine."

"That is what I love about your nation. Such a wonderful sense of humor."

"Text me your address. I'll mail you a copy."

"I'll do that."

"I'm so glad to hear your voice."

"We're Scots," he said. "We're loyal."

Toward the end of summer, Toby drove up to Belle Harbor one evening when Jennifer was out of town at a conference. He'd come straight from work, clad in his company logo T-shirt, a bandana around his neck, cargo pants, work boots. Her handsome son.

For years, Emma's words about heartbreak had haunted Catharine. Part of her always waited for the worst, and it didn't happen. It never would. Toby never broke her heart.

"You know what I realized this week?" Catharine asked as they sat together in the kitchen before dinner. "I was younger than you are now when we first came up here."

Toby took a sip of his beer. He gazed at her with bemusement. "So whose idea was it to move to the end of the earth?"

"Me." Catharine smiled. "I always loved Belle Harbor. I convinced Dad to buy the house. The Money Hole."

Toby said, "I think he loved it here, too."

"Do you?"

"As much as he loved anything."

Catharine said, "That makes me sad."

Toby added, "That's not how it sounds. That Dad didn't love anything. He loved you. And me."

"Of course he did. We loved each other. We always did."

They drifted into quiet.

"I wanted to go for a walk down to the cove. Before it gets dark," Toby said. "Is that okay?"

"Of course. I'll get started on dinner."

The phone rang. Catharine was breathless when she answered on the third ring. She saw it was Toby. "Are you okay?"

"Mom." He laughed. "Not every call is an emergency."

"When did I get this way?"

"You've always been this way," Toby teased.

"You're right."

"I was thinking—" he began.

"What?"

"Do you still have Dad's ashes?"

His mother didn't reply. "Of course," she finally said. "We never did decide where."

"How about now?"

"Now?"

"Let's let him go. I think it's time."

"Where are you?"

"I'm watching a sailboat out in the cove."

"It will take me a few minutes."

Toby watched his mother pick her way down the rocky path a little while later, her bright orange beach bag slung across her shoulder. The strands of gray in her hair glinted silver in the sun. Approaching sixty, she was still a beautiful woman.

"A beach bag?" Toby laughed.

"I'm not going to march down the street clutching an urn to my chest."

"That's too bad." Toby smiled. "There's an image."

He was seated on a rocky outcrop. His mother lowered herself beside him. "Picture catty Mrs. B. tooling past in her Mercedes, rolling down her window. *Are those someone's ashes?*"

"Or the evening crime patrol driving by."

"I still see the nosy one cruising by. Like when you were in high school. What is there for the town to keep daily tabs on down here?"

Toby thought again of Bree's arrest. He snuck a glance at the urn and felt a pang of guilt. "I guess we shouldn't be making jokes."

His mother turned somber. "No."

"So what do we do?"

"I don't know." Catharine shook her head. "I've never scattered anyone's ashes before. I guess we could do it by the handful," she said after a minute. "Or climb down the rocks a little farther and submerge the urn in water. Let the tide carry him away."

"I like that idea," Toby said.

"You'd have to be the one to do it. I think it's too slippery for me down at the edge."

Toby reached for the ashes and she hesitated, then held them straight out with both hands. Toby led the way, and they clambered down to the rocky ledge where the tide lapped against the shore. His mother stopped a few feet behind him.

"We should say a prayer," she said.

She shut her eyes and Toby did the same. When she looked up, he opened the container and handed her the lid. Kneeling at the water's edge, he turned the urn over and held it beneath the water like a baptism rite. The current of starry bits and chunks that had been his dad swirled away beneath them for a while before being pulled out into the cove, a stream of gray dissipating with each incoming wave. He filled the empty urn with seawater a few more times and poured it out, then placed it back inside the beach bag.

Toby got to his feet and put an arm around his mother. She circled hers around his waist. She leaned her head on his shoulder. "What do you think? Is this the place he would have wanted?"

Toby thought of his father coming down here in his pajamas and bathrobe that final June night so many years before. The spot where he used to take Toby fishing, though they never caught anything. The cove where they would sometimes come to watch the sunset, on those rare nights he wasn't too tired after work. "He always liked this spot," Toby said.

"He did." His mother looped her arm in Toby's, and together they made their way home.

After dinner, Toby remembered that he had something for her in his car. "Jennifer gave me a book to bring you. She found it in a box last week. It's the book she told me about that day we first met, from the used bookstore in Somerville. Your poems."

When Catharine opened it, she saw it was the copy she'd given the bride on her honeymoon. How many years ago? Could it really be eighteen? Catharine saw her still, so bright and hopeful. "I remember that week," she said. "The two of them used to twirl around on the willow swing." Catharine paused. "That poor willow."

She stared at the date of her inscription. September 7, 2001. She turned to Toby. "I didn't remember that part. That it was the same week." She closed the book and stared out the window. "That seems like another world now. The Time Before."

"I remember how scared I was that morning," Toby said. "About Dad. Watching TV all afternoon. Waiting for him to call."

They fell silent.

"I've been thinking," Toby started, then stopped. He rotated his beer bottle. Catharine wasn't sure that he'd go on. "I wonder if you've ever considered—maybe it's time you should move back to the city."

"I have thought about it," Catharine said, feeling guilty to admit this. "I have."

Sell the house in Belle Harbor? The idea didn't seem as radical as it once had. If she moved back to the city, she'd be closer to Toby and Jennifer. The new baby. A grandchild. How could she be a grandmother when part of her was still sitting on the steps of Widener, reading her book, Tom Osborne running up two stairs at a time to meet her.

"You should do it," Toby said.

"I might." Catharine tried to picture herself in that life, a different life, a city life. "I know I'd always miss Belle Harbor."

"You could live in the cottage a month each year," Toby said.

Toby hadn't sold the place after he fixed it up after the storm. He rented it out for an outrageous amount to an older academic couple who came up from New York for the summer and returned in September. Catharine often saw them on the deck reading books and sipping wine, just as she'd envisioned when she and Tom first moved to Fairview Road. Now, his mother told him, the adjacent cottage was heaven. A miracle, a quiet couple, after all those chaotic years.

Catharine laughed out loud. "I'd be a summer person!"

"You know I'll give you a special rate, Mom."

"I'll think about it, Toby. I will," she said. She took a deep breath, trying to summon a different life, a new one. "Only—if I move back to the city," Catharine asked after a while, "what will happen to this house?"

Toby thought for a moment and said, "Other people's stories."

CHAPTER 19

Cloudbreak

THE IMPULSIVE PROMISE she'd made to Gavin, the idea of printing another chapbook, wasn't new. Catharine had been thinking about it for a while before he contacted her that summer. Their conversation had finally given her the reason to do it.

Over the years, it had seemed enough to Catharine for several of her poems to appear in print. It was the writing itself that sustained her. The last few months, it seemed past time. The surreal image of her beating heart told her this. Tomorrow was no longer a given.

She gathered the work she'd published and pages of poems still languishing in notebooks to discover she did indeed have a book. Several books. But for now, there could be one.

On a cool afternoon in September she took the commuter rail to Boston—Tom's old train, the scenery he passed every day, the woods and shoreline, the outlying towns. North Station to the screeching Red Line from Park Street to Harvard Square.

People hurried through the Square at the end of the day. Decades ago, she and Tom were one of those young couples. Beyond the tall windows of Harvard Book Store she glimpsed the brick arch to the Yard across the street, the Mass. Ave. campus entrance she'd dashed through hoping to surprise him at work. The night of the fire.

Now, she stood before the Espresso Book Machine at the back of the store, following the instructions for the print-on-demand machine. More amazing technology. All that was required was to upload her thumb drive, hit a button, print a copy.

In that moment with the data stick already in her hand, Catharine paused. Something was missing. She hadn't written a dedication. She wasn't sure why she'd waited until now. At first, she couldn't decide what it should be and then it seemed easier to go ahead without one.

The end-of-day crowd hurried past outside the windows. Catharine heard the hour chime from the Catholic church across the way, the sound of time passing, the sound unchanged since they listened in their little Bow Street café long ago.

It came to her then. Catharine knew what to say.

She found the file for *Cloudbreak* on her laptop. She typed the words and hit save, then loaded the computer file onto the thumb drive and then the machine. Where had this new world come from? The operation quickly sprung to life, gears whirring.

In a few minutes, a warm newly printed copy of her book fell into her hands, the cover an image Tom had photographed years before. She found it on one of the rolls of undeveloped film he left in the toolbox with his notebooks. A tidepool after a storm. A starfish clinging to the surface of a barnacled rock, a blue mussel shell, the reflection of sun and clouds in the cove at the end of Fairview Road, the place where Tom died, the place they'd set him free.

She opened the first bound copy of *Cloudbreak* and read what she'd written:

For Tom.

SHARONA JACOBS

L.H. FINIGAN is a Cape Ann novelist and playwright whose first book, *Love and War*, was an IndieReader Discovery Award finalist. Her fiction and essays have appeared in newspapers and literary journals across the country. Several of her short plays have been staged in and around Boston, including twice at the acclaimed Boston Theater Marathon.

www.lhfinigan.com